Chain of Spring Love

Chain of Spring Love

Robert Bwire

Africana Homestead Legacy Publishers
Cherry Hill, New Jersey

Africana Homestead Legacy Publishers, Inc.
811 Church Rd., Ste 105
Cherry Hill, New Jersey, 08002 USA
www.ahlpub.com
contact: editors@ahlpub.com

Published August 2011.

Printed and bound in the United States of America.
This paper meets the requirements of ANSI/NISO Z39.48-1992 (R 1997)
Permanence of Paper.

Library of Congress Cataloging-in-Publication Data

Bwire, Robert.
 Chain of spring love / Robert Bwire.
    p. cm.
 Summary: "Uhuru settles in Rotterdam, with a geology degree from a
European university and hope for a career at Royal Chelloil. But rejection
and life as illegal alien, working odd jobs to support his family in Uganda,
follows. As gardener for Inge at House of Java, her love tests Uhuru's
marital fidelity; her rebuffed suitor seals his fate"--Provided by publisher.
 ISBN 978-0-9831151-8-2 (alk. paper) -- ISBN 978-0-9831151-9-9 (pbk. :
alk. paper)
1. Ugandans--Netherlands--Fiction. 2. Illegal aliens--Fiction. 3.
Rotterdam (Netherlands)--Fiction. I. Title.
 PR9130.9.B89C48 2011
 823'.92--dc23
                            2011025207

Front cover photo credit: 14ktgold/Bigstock.com

To Domitula Aoko and Romanus Masiga

Zet ze uit de Kerk", dus roept ge luid.
"zet liever gij Uw kerk wat uit!"

"Throw them out of the Church," you loudly proclaim.
But why don't you expand your Church!

(P.A. de Genestet, Dutch poet, 1829-1861)

Contents

Acknowledgments   ix

Chapter 1 The telephone call   1

Chapter 2 Pleasure in illegality   25

Chapter 3 Meeting the employer   51

Chapter 4 Pledge not honored   73

Chapter 5 Friends deliver a verdict   95

Chapter 6 Mutual love   129

Chapter 7 The demise of illegality   153

Epilogue   177

About the Author   181

Acknowledgments

A special thank you is extended, with utmost gratitude, to Nelly, Annelore and Tom, for the continued patience and encouragement. The support of Carolyn C. Williams and her excellent team at AHLP has by no small measure been invaluable, and to them I am profoundly indebted.

Chapter 1 The telephone call

She fretted that her new, bright floral sundress would become wet. So she ran as fast as her tall legs could carry her, which, as she helplessly had to concede, wasn't quick enough to escape the rain. The rain had begun as a playful drizzle of little significance before suddenly quickening up pace to turn into a fully-fledged mid-afternoon tropical storm. Mapenzi thought of breaking her run to ransack through her handbag to retrieve a headscarf to protect hair that had just undergone delicate styling from Elegant Hair Center's new hairdresser, Rosa, a talkative petite woman who had kept her enthralled for a good two hours with tales of matrimonial disquiet.

"Caught that filthy rat red-handed on the kitchen floor," Rosa had said. The rat in question was her husband, a foreman at a cooking oil mill who worked shifts. On this particular occasion, he was supposedly in bed sleeping soundly since he had put in long nocturnal hours on the factory floor.

"With another woman, no doubt?" Mapenzi asked. What else could make a woman so mad to the extent that she deemed it perfectly justifiable to refer to her husband as a distasteful rodent, an unappetizing piece of vermin?

Rosa confirmed it was a woman so repugnant that the very thought of her elicited an urge to puke. She was sure her husband had spied on her, Rosa went on. Once convinced that Rosa had irreversibly hopped onto a minibus, joining the daily exodus of the employed as they left the outskirts and headed to the city's offices and factories, his impatience was such that he wasted little time tearing off his lover's garments. The philanderers had no knowledge that she had removed her wedding ring before peeling green plantains and placed it on the kitchen table, something she had done the previous evening. For her husband insisted on a warm meal each morning when he returned from the night shift.

"I, too, remove my ring whenever performing such household chores," Mapenzi said with apparent delight. She thrilled in the knowledge of following practical logic.

"Once the sticky green plantain sap gets on the ring, it is quite a fight to have it off," conceded a lumpish woman in a styling chair, head under the cap of a hair steaming machine.

Rosa had spat her anger as she expertly shook a bottle and squirted a generous amount of shampoo onto her cupped right palm. "That accursed woman is a bitch! She baby-sits for our neighbors. Now, while on my way to work, I noticed I had left my wedding ring on the table. I made haste and returned home. That is how I found those two panting away the morning! I would have castrated him but for the bluntness of the knife." Rosa gently washed Mapenzi's long curly hair. Mapenzi could not imagine how those gentle hands that soothingly rubbed foamy shampoo into her hair and tenderly massaged her scalp were capable of an act so crude and brutal.

Mapenzi was intrigued. "So what punishment did you mete out?"

Rosa was clearly enjoying the attention. "He is a mighty huge man." She kept quiet for a second or two to allow the half dozen women in the hair salon a brief moment to contemplate the significance of her husband's size, which was all the better to appreciate the heroism of her subsequent blitzkrieg. She then coughed and cleared her throat before pronouncing casually, "But I slapped him, alright. Not once, and not twice … repeatedly with all my might. Told him to fight back and even kill me if he so wished." Rosa stopped her narration which she delivered in a tone of self-congratulation, took one or two animated steps backwards and wriggled her wasp-like waist, clearly enjoying the whispers of admiration and grunts of approval that this show of feminine chivalry elicited among the women in the room. "The coward never raised a hand! Aha, you should have seen his manhood! It was as limp as a toy rubber snake left to dangle on a dying tree branch." This attracted much laughter from the women in Elegant Hair Center.

Rosa's chatter did not interfere with the speed and efficiency with which she executed her work that amazed Mapenzi and had certainly bewildered many others before. At three o'clock she was done with Mapenzi's hair. "Keep it dry for at least one hour or so."

Mapenzi smiled at herself in the full-length mirror amidst ohs and ahs of admiration from women eagerly waiting their turn in the styling chair.

But who had counted on the rain when Mapenzi, a satisfied smile playing on her lips, left Elegant Hair Center and blinked rapidly as she adjusted to the bright sunlight outside on the busy street? As the rain came pelting down on her hair, Mapenzi could not help reflecting on the brutality and inconsideration of fate. Why it hadn't rained the day before when she had nowhere to go was beyond her ken. And as much as she was tempted to open her handbag to retrieve a headscarf, she dismissed the idea as soon as it crossed her mind. She realized it was a futile enterprise, as good as sheltering under an acacia tree in face of an unrelenting storm. What she needed, she ruefully observed, was an umbrella. She did have one but had not foreseen the necessity of carrying it about. And as if to confirm her folly, at that moment Mapenzi's gaze came to rest upon a chic-looking woman in blue stretch jeans and a baggy white shirt with shirttail hem. The woman, unflustered by the rain and totally disinterested in poor townsfolk scuttling to the relative safety of shop awnings across the road, had an umbrella triumphantly held over her by a bored-looking man in tattered clothes and a mean hard look. She was opening the door of a white Land Cruiser, a monstrous object of affluence unsullied by the muddy waters flowing in the street. *Most probably a wife of a ruling party apparatchik,* Mapenzi thought. This thought was not without a sense of envy, whose intensity increased as Mapenzi noticed another street porter, evidently undernourished, arranging the elegant woman's shopping (it was in expensive looking colorful foil embossed carrier bags) on the back seat. Then she quickly revised her assessment of the woman:

more like a mistress of a ruling party bigwig. The conviction that the woman in question was some man's mistress cheered her a bit. It was a kind of a moral victory for her since she despised anybody in an illicit relationship. Mapenzi was almost violently faithful to her husband, and she never doubted that that devotion could not be mutual. Ignoring the Land Cruiser woman who had momentarily held her interest, Mapenzi looked left and right, and seizing the brief moment of absence of cars racing down the road, she darted across Colonel Pokoto Street to relative safety.

Mapenzi was totally soaked when she finally made it under the awning in front of Watoto Inc. store where people huddled together like half-fed cattle that had exchanged the vastness of green pastures for the narrow confines of a cow-dung littered kraal. A faded wooden signboard above the entrance of Watoto Inc. emphatically proclaimed that this was home of the specialists in children's wear since 1972. This brazen defiance of reality and unrepentant defense of myth never ceased to puzzle and, indeed, disturb Mapenzi. For all her twenty-one years of living in Kampala, Mapenzi had known Watoto Inc. as anything but a children's apparel store. It had once prided itself as Kampala's premier stationery shop. That was before every other shop owner in Colonel Pokoto Street awakened to the reality of generous profits from stocking up foolscap paper and ball point pens. Shying away from the stiff competition, Watoto Inc. had reinvented itself as a quality grocery. The new identity didn't last long because of lower prices down at Owino market, forcing Watoto Inc.'s astutely innovative owner, a one Fox Taifa, to redefine his business model. It became a bureau de change, cashing on government's liberalization of the currency market after scrapping laws that had, for decades, made it a serious crime to carry foreign currency in one's pockets. Now, on this Tuesday mid-afternoon, the delicious smell of cooking goat meat, roasting chicken, and burning rice mingled with the sickening odor of evaporating sweat from wet bodies reminding

4

Mapenzi and her fellow refugees on the crowded veranda that Watoto Inc. was a restaurant that specialized in local cuisine. If Mapenzi had had the opportunity of seeing Fox Taifa's business card, she would have read the following golden engraved inscription: "Mr. Fox Taifa PLE Cert., CEO and Chairman, Watoto Inc., Specialists in Children's Wear." Truth of the matter was that he had stayed long enough in elementary school as attested by the Primary Leaving Examination Certificate (PLE Cert) proudly displayed behind his name as if it were the Nobel Prize in managing African economies. However, his knowledge of matters pertaining to children's clothes was, we must regrettably concede, as dismal as a monkey's mastery of tailoring.

"Phew!" whistled a short and stockily built man in greasy khaki overalls standing next to Mapenzi, cashing in on the sense of eager camaraderie that can only arise among humans in face of a natural disaster of staggering magnitude. Mapenzi just stared ahead, not sure the man had addressed her. Cars whizzed past, driving into puddles and bathing those standing close to the sidewalk in muddy water before vanishing round the corner where the exercise was repeated with gusto.

"Fucking bastards!" a woman dripping with water cursed. "Look at their ugly butts caressing comfortable seats in cozy air-conditioned cars and tearing through the street in total disregard of the unfortunate poor!"

"Their time will come." This embittered utterance emanated from a man embedded somewhere in the thick crowd. To this pronouncement there were many assenting voices, although Mapenzi was at a loss as to what the man exactly meant by this veiled threat.

"Tell you, I didn't even see the dark clouds. Happened like lightning," the man in overalls addressed Mapenzi. And just before the last words rolled off the tip of the man's tongue there was a flash of lightning and then a rumbling thunder that sent everybody talking at once.

The man in overalls was determined to engage the rather aloof Mapenzi into conversation. "Must have struck something terribly massive." And the matter-of-fact manner of his voice and the manner in which he opened his eyes round and wide suggested he had in mind something of the gravity of a mountain being split into two. Mapenzi could have chosen to continue ignoring him but this time round there was no mistake he was directly addressing her.

"Maybe." Mapenzi shrugged her shoulders and stoically looked ahead into the rain. It was then that she became acutely aware of her wet sundress clinging on her body as the wind swept about her. And rivulets of water ran down her face from wet hair, disheveled by the sudden storm.

"Your face looks familiar." This time Mapenzi ignored the man in overalls.

But he was not the type to give up easily. "Thought I saw you in Owino Market." He leaned unnecessarily towards Mapenzi, as if this movement was totally out of his control and one that must be squarely blamed on the loud-mouthed, bulky man with an unkempt moustache and disheveled goatee standing to his right. So close was he that Mapenzi could hear the excitement of his heart beating above the dull patter of rain on the corrugated iron sheets of the awning. He was extremely filthy, and his proximity made Mapenzi feel ill at ease.

Of course, it would not rain forever; it never did. But the sooner it stopped pouring the better, she reasoned. Otherwise, if it didn't stop soon, she would have to brave the storm and walk right into it. She didn't have much to lose. After all her hair was totally chaotic looking and her dress ugly with wetness. Somehow she had to get away from this stranger intent on seducing her.

"Sorry mister. You can't be more wrong." Then stealing a quick look at the man she emphatically added, "I never go to Owino Market." This last addition was calculated to remind the man that, in spite of sheltering with the hoi polloi in front of Watoto Inc., she was not his social equal. The elegant women of the moneyed class didn't venture into the filth that was Owino

Market, instead choosing to deploy their servants on such unpleasant errands.

If rain had not disturbed her newly done hair and if her sundress did not cling wetly on her body, she was sure her expensive appearance would have placed an insurmountable barrier that no man on that verandah would contemplate beginning to cross.

"Your sister, perhaps," the man said hopefully. At this point Mapenzi realized with utmost horror that the fiend was poised to touch her! In fact, he would have clapped her back in a gesture of familiarity but for the frighteningly hostile look in Mapenzi's eyes which effectively checked his misguided enthusiasm.

"No, you must be mistaking me with Lucy, my ape-like ancestor." She knew this usually sent salacious males thinking twice before trying another of those utterly dull and depressingly predictable obscene tricks on her. The man took it all rather good-humoredly. He laughed hard and long. But the edge of defeat in his laughter echoed louder than the sonorous peals of mirth. Well, he must have thought to himself it was worth trying. *Maybe it had worked for him the last time round, and he had managed to lay a decent girl, a seamstress perhaps,* thought Mapenzi.

———

As soon as Mapenzi noticed that the rain had turned into a lazy drizzle, she quickly hurried off. And as she walked on the muddy pavement with pools of rain water, she reflected on the encounter with the man under the awnings. The entire episode reminded Mapenzi of another unfortunate occasion that she could not easily dispel from her mind.

Once, she had stood in a queue to buy a ticket for the popular Afrigo Band annual end-of-year music extravaganza at Bat Valley Club when fans went amok like starved ants zeroing on food crumbs. She ended up entrapped in the middle of a crowd pushing to get to the ticket window. In the ensuing melee of near anarchy, the man behind her was quick to exploit the situation, unashamedly pressing a hard and eager erection on her.

So forceful was the man's lewd eagerness that it pushed her dress in the cleft of her buttocks. She later said to Mirembe Hatono, a childhood friend and cousin to her husband, "It felt as if a wide-bore drill was making a large hole through the fabric of my dress. I had to throw away that soiled dress, just couldn't stand the sight of it anymore." She had repeatedly screamed an ineffectual, "Beast, keep off me!" But her spirited protest was promptly lost in the din. Mapenzi could have lunged herself at the fellow, who grinned at her discomfort and was probably on the verge of a massive ejaculation. She itched to claw her repugnancy into his amorous skin, covering it with bleeding scratch marks. It was not to be given her paralysis hemmed in as it were by the excited crowd whose singular focus was on the precious tickets that would give them entry to listen to Afrigo Band's lead vocalist's ethereal voice. The agonizing experience was particularly painful as she realized her physical weakness at a time when she needed to defend her dignity and preserve her integrity as a woman and mother. Albeit that no physical penetration had taken place, Mapenzi perceived the entire episode as rape at the hands of a monstrous brute in broad daylight.

Mapenzi walked the entire length of Colonel Pokoto Street before turning left, towards the General Post Office. She went past Constitutional Square, crossed the busy Old Port Bell Road junction with Entebbe Road, with its hundreds of street hawkers displaying an assortment of bangles, chains, necklaces, and other such glittering trinkets of dubious quality but nonetheless attracting the fancy of countless town folk. A passing look at the dials of the clock on Queen's Tower, some seventy yards or so on her left, proclaimed in all afternoon splendor and majesty that it was quarter to eleven (day or night, take your pick). Mapenzi didn't give the dials further thought. For as long as she could remember, the clock had been in defiant mood, insisting on perpetuation of the status quo irrespective of a desire by mankind to move on in time and space. Why that clock had never been repaired was beyond her! She supposed it didn't take much to repair it, but maybe the exercise was more technically involved than her simple mind assumed. She looked at her watch, an elegant thing that her husband, Uhuru, had dispatched to her all the way from Europe by registered mail, arriving just in time for her thirty-fourth birthday the previous year. It was approaching four o'clock. She told herself it was as well that it had rained; otherwise, she would have turned up rather early at Mirembe's where she had an appointment for four-thirty.

—

"I wonder how the security guards manning the Sementi Tower's gate ever let me through. Aren't I a total disgrace!" Mapenzi was looking at her dress that was now dry but badly crumpled. She had just been ushered into Mirembe's office, a spacious square room from where one had a good view of the activities on Old Port Bell Road (Queen's Tower wasn't visible), on the second floor of Sementi Towers by the secretary, Bulenda, a stoutly built woman with heavy make-up. The floor was covered in red carpet, and the redness was of a hue that reminded Mapenzi of the carpets that are usually rolled out for visiting dignitaries. An entire wall was lined with law books, giving the room a charming scholarly intensity.

"Wouldn't it have been odd if you were not about to crumble!" Mirembe teased. She rose from her chair and stretched out her arms in readiness for an embrace as Mapenzi walked over to greet her. The two women met halfway in the large office and embraced with the warmth and sincerity of people that have been friends since they could care to remember.

Mirembe was Mapenzi's most trusted friend. Mirembe was a lawyer (specialty corporate law) with Gomba & Katwe, Barrister and Solicitor. She wore an expensive pink v-neck dress with bell sleeves. It was a dress that Mapenzi hadn't seen her wearing before. Mapenzi inquired if it was a new dress, and Mirembe said she had owned the dress for one or two years. She didn't recall how long exactly, but quickly added that she didn't fancy the dress that much. "I think it makes me look plump."

Mirembe, who in keeping up with fashion in the glossy European women magazines she subscribed to, was as thin as a reed. Mapenzi reassured her she wasn't plump, and swore the dress was cheerfully delightful. "You look gorgeous, my dear."

"Thank you, Mapenzi," Mirembe smiled affably. She knew that she was as slim as the top models that peopled *Vogue* and *Marie Claire* but all the same confirmation of this fact delighted her immensely and she glowed in the knowledge of having a body so desirous. Mirembe looked outside through the large glass windows. "The thunderstorm gave me quite a fright. I was all over the place on my knees like a handyman, fumbling to unplug the computer and printer cords from the electrical mains."

"I was more worried of being struck by the lightning. Sheltered at Watoto Inc. Looked like all the town's urchins were there."

"How dreadful!"

Mapenzi and Mirembe shared a common disgust for street urchins, whose number seemed to be increasing by the day. Mirembe often said that she didn't think much of street urchins and other idlers that spent their time on the city streets, whiling away the daylight with hours of gossip under shop awnings. "Do sit down, my dear. I'll ask Bulenda to bring us some tea right away."

When Bulenda brought in the tea, Mapenzi accepted it with pleasure. She waited for the secretary to close the door behind her before starting to narrate the afternoon's ordeal in front of Watoto Inc.

"It is annoying enough to have one's hair disheveled by rain," Mapenzi said in way of summary, "It is tragedy to have an afternoon spent in company of men trying to lay you!"

"That is your classical male in his entire primitive aggressiveness and simple stupidity."

"Yes, in all his shocking obscenity." Mapenzi added two cubes of brown sugar to her tea and stirred slowly.

"I suppose the khaki overall chap thought the drumming of the rain on the corrugated iron sheets must cloud your feminine judgment, making you unwittingly prone to embrace new social relationships of a nature calculated to satisfy a lustful and devious human need!" They found themselves laughing at this assessment. Then Mapenzi inquired about Mirembe's work. And to her relief, for she often felt guilty coming to Mirembe's office when she was absorbed in some complicated legal work that demanded her undivided attention, Mirembe reassured her that it was relatively quiet at the moment. She said she was currently finalizing a joint venture contract for an international client, but there was plenty of time to do that.

"How is Juliana, that sweet angel?"

Juliana was Mapenzi's daughter. She was five going on to six. Juliana had been initially christened Harriet. But after a few months of living in the Netherlands, Uhuru had insisted that his daughter's name had to be changed to Juliana. There had been a heated argument, with Mapenzi fighting against a change of name. After all, she argued rather forcefully, Harriet was laden with singular significance. She had named the child for her deceased sister, who had fallen to the ravages of AIDS. But Uhuru was in no mood to humor departed relatives, let alone compromise. He wanted his child named after royalty, and Juliana was just that one name that captured the spirit of monarchism. No amount of counter argument could move Uhuru from his obsession. Mapenzi couldn't understand her husband's sudden hobnobbing with monarchists since he had passed harsh judgment and spared no condemnation of the hereditary rulers of his village in the past. When she put this to him, he said rather mysteriously, "Our William of Nassau, Prince of Orange, was first a Catholic, then a Lutheran, and died an unbending Calvinist. I, too, have a right to change my political convictions."

So after going through the early part of her life answering to Harriet the child was re-christened Juliana, after a Dutch princess. All Mapenzi's friends and family had said Juliana was such a sweet name, which left her confused. Wasn't it these same

11

people that had passed similar indiscriminate judgment when she had chosen to call the child Harriet? Mapenzi was now telling Mirembe how brilliant and cheerful Juliana was at the moment.

"My house would be one dull place without that little darling around."

"Is she still enjoying her new school?"

"That school is the best thing that ever happened to her!"

Juliana had recently enrolled in primary one at Three Piglets Primary School, the finest and most exclusive primary school in the city. Only the rich could afford its exorbitant school fees that had to be paid in dollars and not the local shillings. Payment in euro could be negotiated, but it involved a lengthy discussion with the school principal, a woman of unbending scruples and unyielding principles, acquired, it was said, in Switzerland where she had lived for years as a wife of a diplomat. It cost Mapenzi four hundred and eight dollars each school term. Since there were three school terms in a year, this added to a total sum of one thousand two hundred and twenty-four dollars that excluded miscellaneous costs for school milk and other such luxuries as are found in a school of such fine pedigree.

"I must pop in soon. Hard to believe I haven't seen her in almost one month."

"Seven weeks to be precise."

Mirembe was alarmed. "Has it been that long? Girl, oh girl, doesn't time fly?" Indeed, she had last seen Juliana seven weeks earlier when Mapenzi had asked her to drive them to see an ophthalmologist on the other side of town, a man that was said to have had a lucrative practice in London, on Harley Street. Mapenzi had been worried about the child's eyesight when Juliana had begun complaining of itchy eyes. It turned out that she had an allergy of sorts that disappeared in the next few days and then after they had paid the ophthalmologist twenty dollars in consultation fees.

Mirembe said it would be a good thing if they could find a date to go out shopping together. Mapenzi proposed the coming Saturday. However, Mirembe couldn't make it on that day. There was an office party, and all the important lawyers in town had been invited. She said it would be such a terrible thing to miss the party that was crucial for networking.

Mirembe leaned back in the chair and crossed her legs. "How about Sunday evening? We could go down to the National Theater. Alex Mukulu's 'Forty Years of Bananas' is showing. And after that we could eat something."

"Not Watoto Inc., I pray?" Mapenzi laughed.

"Certainly not!" Mirembe assured, laughing as well. "I definitely have no appetite for bull trotters. And I do not fancy using my hands to eat steamed plantains and boiled goat meat."

"Neither do I."

"China Wall, then?"

"Chopsticks, my dear!" Mapenzi enthused. "Isn't it quite decent and trendy? Gather the clientele list reads like who is who in Kampala glamour-land."

"The Kibandas were spotted at China Wall last week." Mirembe told Mapenzi that she had read this piece of newsworthy information in the gossip column of the *Savannah Socialites*, a local weekly magazine of extraordinarily poor quality, but, nonetheless, a worthwhile read if the aim was to while away the hot Saturday afternoon at a lakeside hotel. The Kibandas were well connected with the political establishment and their wealth was legendary in the city. They were probably the richest family in the country. Their business interests included two national newspapers, a copper mine, a game park, numerous food processing plants, a chain of luxury hotels, and supermarkets. Some mean-spirited people whispered the Kibandas didn't shy away from less respectable enterprises; they were reportedly deep into smuggling drugs and illicit diamonds from a neighboring war-torn country, and it was rumored they had won the lucrative contract of operating the portable toilet that accompanied the president whenever he traveled around the country. Not to be outplayed by Mirembe, Mapenzi reeled off a list of the Kampala famous that patronized the newly opened Chinese Wall restaurant opposite the Houses of Parliament.

"Chinese food is great, though it is a real pity we don't have McDonalds," Mapenzi said, and then showing her considerate nature, added, "Shouldn't we ask Rachel to join us?" Rachel was another childhood friend. She was a clerical officer at the Ministry of Justice.

"Splendid idea, my dear! She looked rather tired the last time I saw her … like anemic or something."

"You haven't heard then?"

"What are you talking about?"

"Her fifth child is on the way."

"You are telling me!" Mirembe half-sat and half-jumped off the chair.

Mapenzi lowered her voice to a conspiratorial tone. "Missed two periods, she told me."

The sound of automatic gunfire tore through the tranquility of Mirembe's office, and the women were momentarily thrown in a state of near panic, as they quite forgot all about Rachel's fifth pregnancy. However, their confidence returned when they heard the booming male voice of Mr. Frederick Katwe, the senior partner of Gomba & Katwe, Barrister and Solicitor, assuring a scared client, an Indian businessman, in the corridor that the gunshots weren't in the building, but outside. "It is the police shooting at a pickpocket ... happens all the time. I wonder if all that show of excessive force is necessary though. Last time round the bullets went astray, killing a poor child jumping rope in her backyard." It was then that Mirembe and Mapenzi relaxed, and overcoming their initial shock, walked to the huge windows, and while looking at the street below them, also wondered loudly why it was an absolute necessity to use live ammunition in a public street to stop a pickpocket. There was total confusion in the street with people running back and forth, but no sign of the thief or police. Presently, order returned to the streets. Mapenzi was in a way glad that Uhuru was far removed from all this senseless madness, where a man could be killed for something as petty as stealing a bun to feed his hungry children, and God forbid that a stray bullet should kill Uhuru while visiting the city.

—

From time to time, Mapenzi looked at her watch. "He should be ringing anytime now."

"Impatient?" Mirembe delicately sipped her second cup of tea. She was conscious of Mapenzi's repeated glances at her watch.

"Five minutes to go," Mapenzi said with some mortification. She didn't want Mirembe feeling as though she wasn't interested in her company.

"He will ring alright. That is if the certainty of history repeating itself is anything to go by."

"Uhuru is such a dear. Pity he is far away." Mapenzi paused and sighed. "If only I could get a passport! Yes, with a passport it might be easier for me to visit him in Rotterdam. He could send us tickets to visit him each summer. But this …" Mapenzi's voice faltered, and she broke off mid sentence, as if the gravity of contemplating the reality of living separated from her husband was too painful to dwell on any further. Once in a while the unreserved approval of Uhuru's absence that she paraded in public crumbled when she became acutely aware of the unbridgeable distance that separated them.

"It must be hard for him as well, I am sure it is. He has never gotten to see his own daughter, and that must hurt sorely. I wonder what must be going on through Juliana's mind … I mean, having a father that you have never seen."

"Oh, Juliana is quite proud of her father. You shouldn't worry about her. She knows he is out there because of his great love for us. Without the monthly check where would we be? There would be no decent house over our heads and no Three Piglets for Juliana. That much I have tried to impart to her, and it is astonishing how that child comprehends and appreciates her father's sacrifice. It is all very well for you … you have an excellent job." Seeing that Mirembe might misconstrue this reference to her well-paid and secure position as an unreasonable manifestation of resentment and jealousy, Mapenzi quickly added, "Oh, do not misunderstand me, Mirembe. I am so glad you studied hard and earned a law degree. God knows you deserve all the good things you have. All I want to say *is*, now that he is out there fending for me and the child, I do not have to rise up early each morning to balance a basket on my head walking the eight odd kilometers to sell tomatoes or potatoes in Owino market."

"You do miss him, don't you?" Mirembe inquired tentatively. She often wondered how one could manage to remain married to a man physically absent from one's life for six and a half years. In all honesty, she couldn't have cared a straw if Mapenzi had announced to her that she had found a new lover and was forfeiting the marriage. Mirembe looked at the hooded sadness in Mapenzi's eyes and weighed if she shouldn't tell her it was about time she found herself another husband after all. But consideration that she was a woman of independent means, as opposed to Mapenzi, who, though financially secure, had to rely on the earnings of a husband in Europe, stopped Mirembe from proffering advice. Mirembe also suspected Mapenzi would confront her with the classical argument of people living in fear of mortal poverty and distasteful misery justifying their willingness to put up with the intolerable suffering of long separations from spouses, as long as the arrangement guaranteed enough resources to lead a decent life. That much Mapenzi seemed to have made abundantly clear to her.

Mapenzi nodded slowly but resolutely, "Yes, I do miss him. But he gets to ring me, and that in itself gives me enormous happiness and enough strength to go on." In fact, there were moments when she sorely regretted his absence and stood on the verge of asking him to return home. The occasion of Juliana's first christening was one such painful moment. In the conspicuous absence of Uhuru, Mapenzi had to be contented with a godfather: Mirembe's boyfriend, Benga. When all the visitors who had come to the child's christening ceremony had left, and she had finally put her daughter to bed, Mapenzi had lain in her bed and cried long into the dark and lonely night.

———

The telephone rang just as Mapenzi and Mirembe were finishing their tea. One half of Mapenzi wanted to jump at the phone, but her other half that was much stronger and less prone to instinctive knee-jerk reflexes, counseled restraint. It took civilized courage to remain seated in her chair and not be the first to reach for the phone.

Mirembe winked at her friend as she walked to her large smooth mahogany table to answer the phone. "That will be our Dutchman, no doubt."

The women had nicknamed Uhuru the "Dutchman."

———

Two months after his arrival in the Netherlands from a former Soviet bloc country where he had studied geology (Siberian rocks were his territory of specialization), they had reached an understanding that he would ring Mapenzi every first Tuesday of the month. But Mapenzi did not have a telephone. It was extremely fortunate that she could count on Mirembe for the use of her office telephone to receive international calls. Mirembe was such a dear, and she saw no reason why she shouldn't oblige to her friend's request. Besides, Mirembe felt she owed it to her since it was their friendship that had introduced Mapenzi into Uhuru's life, and that relationship had blossomed, maturing into marriage. It is for this reason that Mapenzi found herself in Mirembe's office the first Tuesday of every month without fail.

Uhuru had been faithful, never failing to ring her at five o'clock. There was an arrangement that he would ring between quarter to five and half past five. How Mapenzi looked forward to their monthly fifteen minutes conversation! Waiting for the first Tuesday of the month became a lifeline, an obsession. For a quarter of an hour, the telephone bridged their two worlds. She always planned on telling him lots of things, but as soon as she heard his voice, she quite forgot ninety percent of it. She was unable to articulate all the things so meticulously thought out and rehearsed for days. She would say to herself when she hung up the phone that perhaps the constraints imposed by fifteen minutes in a month were to blame for her inability to effectively articulate what she wanted to say.

Nonetheless, Mapenzi gladly listened to her husband, and through her silence, encouraged him to tell her more of his experience in the rich West, for she knew about this El Dorado through hearsay and television soaps. She thrilled in the notion that indeed her husband lived that life of lavishness, an existence of infinite ease and dizzying comfort. What could she tell him about her world, her life? Nothing much really she surmised. For the vicissitudes as existed he knew about, and then, through personal experience and not hearsay. She was sure if he as much as began to forget, television images of forbidding countenance would refocus his attention to the plight of his suffering kin and kith left behind on a cruel continent. How was it like living out there, she would press? However, he downplayed the sweetness and the sheer beauty of breathing cold wind. When he had once said, "Not easy to scratch a living out here, and I miss the sun," she had attributed that remark to his modesty. How could you yearn for the hot sun when it came down so mercilessly and dulled your senses? Uhuru had told her that he lived in a high-rise building, on the sixth floor, which to her impressionable mind represented the ultimate in modernity. Yes, he had been to McDonalds and had eaten a hamburger! How that bit of information had thrilled her! It amused her extensively when he talked about the Metro and tram, and it was all irresistibly inviting. Last time he had told her about a beauty center where elegant Dutch ladies had their sun-tanned bodies smeared in chocolate to reinvigorate and rejuvenate the aging skin. She had closed her eyes and tried to imagine her body dripping extravagantly with chocolate. Yes, she loved chocolate but not as some form of beauty ointment. It was these tales that left her convinced there was a lot of squandering of plentiful resources, which wasn't a bad thing at all although she also thought it was the height of pompous irresponsibility to look at chocolate as anything else but a titillating delicacy. Infused with the discovery that out there was a world of superfluous wealth, she had made a wish list, which, with positive anticipation, she had eagerly presented to Uhuru.

"Send us a car," Mapenzi had asked Uhuru. She had no reason to suppose her wish wouldn't be granted or be given serious consideration. She had requested this perfume or that dress, and those delightful tributes of her heart's desire Uhuru had promptly dispatched to her by registered mail.

"A car?" Uhuru's face had taken on the horrified contortion of a mortally wounded man asked to perform a Herculean task.

Uhuru was glad for the thousands of kilometers that separated them, placing his face beyond scrutiny. It was with extreme difficulty that he had managed to buy a derelict second-hand bicycle, a Gazelle that had been stolen six days later. Some of the fellows he hung around with suggested he should also steal a bicycle. "Everyone does steal bicycles," they had encouraged. Even if the entire country found the practice commendable, he had his reservations about joining the rank of thieves. He had, therefore, resolutely declined to play along in spite of constant sneers from his friends that it was exactly this kind of pigheadedness that made integration into Dutch society rather impossible. His wife had asked for a car! And she said her preference was a Ferrari! She had seen it on a cover of a glossy magazine borrowed from Mirembe, and she had found it sexy and worth owning for one with a husband in a land where chocolates were rubbed into the skin. Of course, it was worth owning, he reflected with amused patience at his wife's simplicity. Mapenzi had no conception of the reality of an immigrant's life, and indeed, Uhuru realized it was vain trying to correct her erroneous perception borne of ignorance and failure to look beyond the romanticized world of the silver screen and fashionable magazines. She would have been gravely disappointed if he had told her of his daily hardships. He was sure if Mapenzi discovered the truth, a truth that had come upon him the last years with glaring clarity, she would beseech him to give up Europe and return home. Uhuru didn't want to get caught up in such a delicate discussion, especially before realizing his dreams and reaching his goals. But what was it that he hoped to achieve? At what point would he decide he had fulfilled the things he had set out to do for himself and was thus ready to pack his bags and head back to Africa? Unfortunately, Uhuru had no clue. Whenever Mapenzi inquired about his life expecting that he would reinforce the rosy picture in her mind, he became less enthusiastic in describing his surroundings and relationships. And about the Ferrari, without much conviction and a sense of guilt at his falseness, he had mumbled something about trying to do all within his means (he didn't explicitly admit his means were rather strained) to send a car. He was careful not to say it would be a Ferrari, but he didn't explicitly say he couldn't afford the Ferrari, either.

Mirembe limited her brief chat with Uhuru to an exchange of pleasantries of a nature that mainly hinged on the state of the foulness of the Northern Hemisphere's punishing weather. She had once attended a conference in Bergen, Norway, in the winter. The punishing frozen wind tore through her skin, cracking her lips and rendering her fingers and toes paralyzed with an icy numbness. And for the one week she stayed in Norway, she was so totally frozen that she didn't have the ability to shiver from the cold. She told Mapenzi that she had even remained frozen throughout the return flight, and that she was sincerely thankful when the plane finally touched down at Entebbe International Airport, where, to her immense surprise, her body immediately defrosted. The European experience was one she didn't wish to repeat.

Mirembe handed the handset of the cordless telephone to Mapenzi. "For you, my dear. I'll give you a lift home. So there is no legal justification to entertain miserable thoughts of squeezing onto a crowded bus, which would disrupt the joy of the sacred afternoon with the Dutchman."

"Oh, I can take the bus, dear." Mapenzi was deeply touched by her friend's gesture which was so generous and warm.

"Silly. I'll drive you home," Mirembe whispered. She walked out of the room, leaving Mapenzi alone in the large office. Mirembe always left her alone. To talk in all candidness with her husband in an unrestrained stress-free environment, she would tell Mapenzi.

———

They had been talking for seven minutes. That much she could see after stealing a quick glance at her watch. Yes, Mirembe had been right about time flying, Mapenzi reflected. The excitement of talking to Uhuru after so many weeks of patient waiting was overwhelming. It was as if she was meeting him for the first time. His delightful laughter was so real that she had difficulty realizing that he wasn't in the room. She could almost see those white teeth and the mischievous twinkle that he always had in his eyes at moments like these. Her body ached with desire; she longed to touch him, to feel his ebony skin. But, alas! She had to content herself with the sound of his breathing which was so audible above his strong voice. She might have woken up alone each morning, but she believed he was always there, lurking out there, thinking of her every single minute. That recognition and appreciation of his concern for her welfare filled her with enough faith to go on without his physical presence. Oh, to hear him talk and laugh was to be contented with life, Mapenzi decided. He was now telling her about the money he had transferred to her. Three hundred and eighty euro. She was so grateful for his generosity, and she thanked him profusely. He said he would have loved to send much more, and she protested that three hundred and eighty euro was more than she could spend in a month! What would she do with more euro, she asked? "Our beauty salons are still evolving from the Stone Age, else I would use that money to give myself a treat in a chocolate bath!" She laughed.

He laughed, too. "You are so funny, darling."

"Uhuru, my dear, can you smell the scent of the perfume you sent me with the last package?"

"Not exactly," he answered cheerfully. "Perhaps, do get closer to the phone."

They laughed at their playfulness, as they indulged in the sheer delight of their flirtatiousness. She had so many things on her mind that she wanted to share with Uhuru, but there was simply not enough time to recount all the events of the past month. So she decided that some of the issues that required highlighting would be kept for next time, and she found herself saying, "Isn't it so terrific to hear your voice."

"Thrilled to hear your heartbeat, my darling Mapenzi." Then he inquired about what she was wearing. Mapenzi dressed up in beautiful clothes whenever she came to talk to her husband. And this she did, not so much for her own aesthetic considerations (true, she was a woman of profound taste), but for the benefit of a husband that couldn't see what she was wearing.

"A beautiful but ruined cotton sundress," she said half-jokingly. "And if you must know my newly done hair is a total mess."

"Whatever happened, darling?"

"Caught up in the rain on my way here." It had been four months when she last raised the matter of the car, and she realized now was the time to gently remind him. "If I had a car, my hair would never have been ruined in the first place and that lovely dress would not be covered in hideous mud." But to her horror, she realized their time was up and that Uhuru couldn't brief her on the Ferrari's progress. Uhuru was saying, "Take care, honey, and give thousands of kisses to baby Juliana from me with love. Tell her that Daddy misses her very much. Please don't forget to go down to Western Union to withdraw the money. Bye-bye." And his voice, which a while ago was so close and tangible, retracted into an imperceptible, but agonizingly decisive nothingness.

"Bye-bye, darling," Mapenzi said limply, as the phone with a finite silence louder than her husband's laughter went dead in her hands. Then she realized with much horror that she was frightened to be alone. She felt quite miserable, as the clutch of loneliness tightened its grip on her. *Yes, fifteen minutes are but a very short time in a woman's life*, Mapenzi thought bitterly. The money that he faithfully sent each month helped her afford a life of comfort, a lifestyle that was envied by many in the city. But was that what she wanted in life? Was it worth enduring his absence? Oh, how she longed to continue their conversation without the barrier of separation, and look him in the eye, explore his body, and feel secure in his laughter. Assailed with profound depression and resignation, she whispered, "Uhuru, do return home soon. Then we shall not be separated till death do us part." She took a deep breath and hesitantly pressed the OFF button of the handset before carefully replacing it back in its base. And for no apparent reason, she was struck with a terror that she might never see him alive. As hard as she tried, Mapenzi could not shake off that fatalistic feeling. In fact, the more she tried to ignore it, the more it took a deeper conviction. Stress, she managed to rationalize.

Chapter 2 Pleasure in illegality

The book's title held out so much promise for one such as Uhuru. It was aptly called, *An illegal immigrant's guide to paid work. A beginner's guide to work in the Netherlands*. The book was the work of Johannes de Lange, *Rotterdam Weekly Herald* columnist, publicist, and champion of Rotterdam city's downtrodden. Greg Okafor, a once upon a time illegal alien from Africa but since turned city of Rotterdam burger, had recommended the book to Uhuru. Greg was the official tenant of apartment number 741 E in Prof. A.S. van Vredeman, which Uhuru and another chap, Pierre Kalongo, who had immigrated from sub-Saharan Africa and had obtained all the necessary legal papers that allowed him to live and work in the Netherlands, sub-rented. Pierre had trained as a civil engineer in Africa, but since his qualifications weren't recognized in Europe, he found himself working at the Post Office, sorting mail.

"Only way to get yourself a decent paying job," Greg said, "is to get hold of Johannes de Lange's book."

Uhuru had been for weeks out of odd jobs usually reserved for one of his station in life, and the weariness of uncertainty had begun gnawing at his restless soul. Of course, Greg wanted him to get a steady job, and more so, because Uhuru still owed him the February rent that was one hundred and fifteen euro and fifty cents. They had haggled over the fifty cents, for Uhuru had seen no particular significant reason why the fifty cents wasn't just dropped from the rent. But Greg doggedly insisted, as if the fifty cents stood between him and dire poverty.

Uhuru was skeptical about Johannes de Lange's book. "Aren't you giving too much credit to that book?"

"How do you imagine Okoro got that lucrative job as a security guard?" queried Greg. "He had tried all kinds of things to no avail until some good soul introduced him to the book. It is a step-by-step guide that leads you from the obscurity of illegality to a respectable job."

"Perhaps, I could borrow the book from Okoro," Uhuru mused hopefully.

Greg shook his head. "That will not help your cause. You need the most recent edition. Get a copy, dude. It will help you out of those sweeping and cleaning jobs for a change."

Indeed, Uhuru had hitherto managed to do mostly cleaning jobs. It was mainly in restaurants and bars and the occasional factory floor. It brought in enough money to meet his daily expenditures and still be able to spare hundreds of euro for Mapenzi and baby Juliana. But he still hoped to put his university training to good use. Uhuru had come to the Netherlands especially because a fellow student at his university in a former Soviet bloc country had suggested that with an educational background in geology the chaps at Royal Chelloil would undoubtedly fight over him.

The logical journey to his Great Dutch Dream had been embarked upon six years earlier, and it had taken him four days. There was a tiring bus ride to the Polish border, hitchhiking along the highway, and a rather pleasant time spent in the company of a jovial rotund lorry driver who had given him a lift without asking obtrusive questions as to his motives traveling to Germany. The last hours were spent on an international train bound for the Netherlands. He had arrived in the Netherlands with a lone polyester fabric suitcase of an obscure brand in his hand, an infinite well of hope throbbing in his heart, and close to three thousand United States dollars in his tired-looking leather wallet. The dollars he had saved from earnings as a seasonal laborer. During summer vacation, Uhuru and a group of other non-European students dispersed in the West, in search of temporary work. In fact, he had been to the Netherlands on two previous occasions, one time working in a greenhouse growing champignons and another in one that grew paprika. It was during this stint that he had taken a keen interest in the country, eventually falling in love with the dykes, polders, and canals.

The train had brought him to Rotterdam Central Station, its final destination. He had stood about in the busy train station, thoughts lost in the crowded hall. He had arrived in Rotterdam, but he was at a loss regarding his next move. Now that the possible permanence of his stay looked inevitable, he began looking at his surroundings with focused interest and with significantly deeper observations than the superficial, cursory observations of a naïve tourist or a dreamy seasonal migrant worker. The sight of a homeless man talking to himself like a zombie and a group of rowdy drug addicts led him to rethink his strategy. The spectacle was enough to inspire uncertainty and unleash a fear leading him to conclude that Rotterdam Central Station was not a safe place to spend the next few days. He had to leave urgently and try to find a decent place from where he could chart his strategy to join Royal Chelloil. Uhuru went from street to street, looking for affordable hotel accommodation. Two hours later and on the verge of collapsing from exhaustion, he found himself retracing his steps back to the first hotel that he had rejected because he had thought he would very well find accommodation for far less than the forty euro a night which he had been asked to pay. He stayed for one week. He would probably have stayed much longer if it hadn't been for a fortuitous accident.

As he walked in the street on one chilly morning, he overheard two men speaking in Swahili. His heart had beaten faster on hearing a familiar language. He quickened his pace and caught up with the two. He had thrown away any pretense at modesty, telling them that his was a desperate situation, a steep descent into a cataclysmic end—he had to find alternate cheap accommodation and quick. The state of the housing didn't matter. What he desired most in this world was a habitat that would protect him from the cold, ruthless, and unfriendly Rotterdam streets. Could they help? But they said that they were international students recently arrived in the country and were still befuddled by their new environment, which, thank goodness, they had to endure for just under one year before heading back to the warm climes of the tropics. But he pleaded with them to help him in any way, because at this rate he would run out of money. "Have a heart, dudes," Uhuru stammered. "You surely wouldn't walk away from me with clean consciences and concentrate on your studies knowing that one of your own is hanging out in the cold street, in mortal danger of freezing to death." At this the students had chuckled extravagantly and said he was a jolly funny man. Then one of them said he could take him to a cheap accommodation that he had rejected, on account of the noise and state of near squalor. "Not an atmosphere conducive to reading," the young African scholar had explained to Uhuru. "But seeing you are not a student who has to do coursework, it might just serve your purposes." Indeed, the apartment was derelict, but Uhuru had accepted it with open arms. He would have a bedroom to himself and share other amenities with a group of chaotic and ill-mannered youths. Given the fact it would cost him one hundred and ninety euro a month, it was a bargain he would ill afford not to embrace.

As soon as Uhuru had readjusted himself to his new environment, he judged that the time was ripe to send an open application to Royal Chelloil, drawing their attention to his availability and readiness to serve the industry with dedication and hard work. He particularly stressed his mastery of matters related to Siberian rocks, sealed the envelope with great expectation, and saw to it that the letter got posted by delivering it personally at the busy post office. The letter of rejection was swift in coming, and its message unambiguous and impersonal. Royal Chelloil didn't think much of his training. He was to later hear from other aliens that he had stood no chance, whatsoever, and Royal Chelloil would not have invited him to an interview no matter how many good fucking application letters he wrote. The mere reading of a foreign sounding name was reason enough for a Dutch company to feed a letter of application into a shredder, destroying the well-constructed and savvy epistle of an intelligent mind seeking honest work. After the disappointment of Royal Chelloil, Uhuru had tried his hand at anything that came his way. He got a job as a refuse collector and even worked briefly as a chef's assistant. He thought of driving a taxi, but on learning of the ongoing infighting between two different taxi organizations, he decided not to pursue the matter any further. He preferred operating in the shadows, keeping away from the spotlight. Then he had got a job with a small family cleaning business that was contracted to do the cleaning at Jansen & van Amersfoort, a medium-sized pig abattoir. It was there that he had met Greg. "You must come and stay at my Prof. A.S. van Vredeman apartment. Paying so much for a pigsty! The landlord is ripping you off." Greg had shaken his head in disbelief and clicked his tongue in a musical tone that only Africans could muster. Two days after this offer, Uhuru had moved into the apartment, sharing it with Greg and Pierre.

———

The jolt of the Royal Chelloil rejection letter had come hard and cruel on him. Since then he had lowered his expectations, concentrating on scratching a living from the disadvantage of the very margins of society. He was positively sure that if destiny had not led him to a path of scratching a living in the dark catacombs of illegality, he would have been a workaholic business executive in the oil industry. That mouth-watering six-figure annual income, he had to realistically concede, had completely eluded him. But now Greg had alerted him to this book which he swore was Uhuru's key to a more interesting and respectable job.

"But if the book offers so much," Uhuru reasoned, "why don't you get a copy and get yourself a job? The way I see it, you will need a job sooner than later."

Greg was presently unemployed and had been for the last eight months. He had worked for fourteen uninterrupted years as a boner and slicer at Jansen & van Amersfoort. But because of reorganization at the abattoir, Greg and twenty-two other colleagues had been axed.

"I can boast an impressive employment record. Fourteen years of hard work, and, I dare say, I honestly contributed my share to the benefits that I am currently getting. I don't have any shame whatsoever collecting my monthly benefits check. And in any case once the economy pulls out of recession, I am convinced those fellows at Jansen & van Amersfoort will be looking for boners and slicers. There aren't many around with my experience. Just stop being silly and go down to the bookshop."

The small bookstore in Charlois did not have Johannes de Lange's book. In fact, the elderly bookseller, a slight man with large, restless eyes and a receding forehead, told Uhuru that he had heard of Johannes de Lange (who hadn't in Rotterdam?) and enjoyed very much reading his provocative columns in the *Rotterdam Weekly Herald*.

"There was this article that was a penetrating and balanced criticism of the cabinet's greed. He wrote that a fortnight ago. I can't believe that those ladies and gentlemen are scheming to give themselves a salary rise, especially at a time of economic recession when they are urging everyone to tighten their belts. But Johannes de Lange has given them a piece of his mind, I tell you! And did you read his column, perhaps six or seven weeks ago, when he declared himself among the few remaining courageous souls in this country unwilling to succumb to the current rampant prejudice and xenophobia, recycled from the dark ages of Nazism?" The bookseller chuckled as he ran a dry hand through neatly combed thin gray hair. Anyway, he went on, he wasn't aware that Johannes de Lange wrote books as well.

"What is the title again?" the bookseller asked, with keen interest.

Uhuru looked at the handwritten note in his hands and with a voice quivering with hope spoke up, "An illegal immigrant's guide to paid work. A beginner's guide to work in the Netherlands."

"You aren't illegal, I suppose?". The bookseller intensely studied Uhuru's face. Uhuru cast his eyes to the floor. He didn't like the way in which the man was prying into his private life. One never knew with the natives, Pierre always told Uhuru. They were supposedly good at whistle blowing and ratting on neighbors, a kind of national pastime. Seeing his discomfort, the bookseller quickly added, "If you ask me, we Westerners have screwed up the third world, and we should take responsibility for the mess out there. Now, look at the Hutus wielding machetes and butchering the Tutsis. It is the legacy of colonialism, isn't it? But anyway, you were looking for Johannes de Lange's book. I say, my good fellow, why don't you try Donner?"

Uhuru thanked the old bookseller and made his way to the Lijnbaan to Donner bookshop that was crowded with bookish types as was apt to happen on a Saturday. Unfortunately, he was told that the book was out of stock, but the bookshop expected to have it within a week. He decided to look around, perusing through the newest literary works. A book about Feyenoord caught his attention. He was an ardent supporter of the Rotterdam soccer club. His housemates rooted for Sparta Rotterdam and were fanatical about it. But before he could pick up the Feyenoord book, he saw the latest edition of the *Vorstin*, a magazine that kept him updated on the state of the monarchy and the decadent lives of the royal players. He could not resist buying it.

—

Uhuru sat in the rear car of a half-full tram, the back of his throat itching for a cigarette. He had some distance to go on tram no. 8 which he had taken out of sheer idleness now that the very purpose of his journey to City Center had not amounted to much. He should have been on tram no. 2, but he hadn't seen the urgency to get home quickly. Desperate to light up, he got off the tram, not far off from Erasmus Bridge. With the impatience of an addict who was denied nicotine for weeks, he cupped his hands and lit up a cigarette. He inhaled long and deep. Then for no particular significant reason, he convinced himself that he would walk a circuitous route back to the apartment. It didn't matter much that it would take him almost an hour to get back home. Barely noticing the bustle of the street around him, he walked leisurely, cigarette in hand.

He went past an Indonesian restaurant and avoided crushing into an elderly woman with a walking frame. He found himself thinking about Juliana. Uhuru longed to carry her in his arms and to listen to her telling children's stories. He wondered about what she might be doing at that time. *But why?* he asked himself. She must be out in the street playing with the neighborhood children. He stopped at a toy shop and took enormous pleasure studying a huge brown teddy bear in the display window. Just the kind of toy he would love to dispatch to Juliana. Yes, his lovely Juliana! He had yet to set eyes on her beautiful, angelic face in real life, but he was determined to work hard for her, to give her a life better than the one he had had as a child growing up in the rural African countryside.

There had been many moments of hunger, misery, and desperation back in the village. Although Uhuru was an extremely brilliant pupil, he couldn't take school for granted. His parents never seemed to have enough money to pay his school fees. Nonetheless, through unending sacrifice which at times took the form of the family skipping a meal, his parents had ensured that he had got the right education. Finally, Uhuru had won a government scholarship and ended up at university in a former Soviet state where he embarked on a four-year geology course. His scholarship was generous, providing for an opportunity to travel back to Uganda on three occasions that were at his discretion. He had taken advantage and used the offer. It was six and a half years ago that he had last traveled to his homeland. That trip he had made ostensibly to collect data for his final dissertation, a comparative work of Siberian and the Great African Rift Valley rocks. During that four month stay in Uganda, he had also married his longtime girlfriend, Mapenzi. And how he made the best of that brief period with Mapenzi! When he finally said farewell to his teary wife and boarded the aircraft, an Ilyushin 86, for Europe, Mapenzi was three months pregnant.

Uhuru now reaffirmed his commitment to make up for his long absence by making sure his daughter got all the comfort that he could afford to shower upon her. He thought of stepping into the toy store and purchasing that lovely looking teddy bear. A man with a ponytail dressed in a gray striped Brixton suit and tennis shoes walked past Uhuru, talking loudly on the mobile phone, totally oblivious of any other soul inhabiting the earth. Uhuru disliked these loud-mouthed types with their mobile phones, especially on the tram or Metro. Deciding that fifteen euro was too high a price to pay for a teddy bear, Uhuru made to continue his stroll when he was immobilized.

"Excuse me, boy," a male voice ordered in a tone of unambiguous authority from behind Uhuru. Uhuru turned to look. It was a large policeman wearing a rather stern moustache. And the man of law and order wasn't smiling. He had the roguish mannerisms of a drill-sergeant, and Uhuru was the underdog with no rights, whatsoever.

"Yes," Uhuru stammered, fearing for the worst. Uhuru's palms became moist. He felt the dryness of panic in his mouth and a loud pounding of fear in his chest. He half-closed his eyes and murmured a silent prayer of delivery. He stayed in this country illegally, and the fear of deportation was constantly on his mind. He knew of illegal aliens that had been rounded up and locked up in the Rotterdam Airport deportation center. The conditions were far worse than in a Siberian camp and inmates treated no better than the hardcore criminals that were in the maximum security jail in Vught, so it was rumored. The very thought of being confined for months fighting for one's sanity before unceremoniously being bundled onto a plane back to Africa had a blood curdling effect, and his heart missed a beat or two.

"Police," the man announced rather unnecessarily and extravagantly. "Routine body search, boy. Will you turn to face the wall? I warn you that any form of non-cooperation will be seen as obstruction of a law enforcement officer. Is that clear?" The stern bark of the policeman's voice left Uhuru in no doubt that given the slightest opportunity, this man could crack his skull. Uhuru's face relaxed a little because he now understood he wasn't being stopped for deportation. It was one of those routine police body searches, supposedly conducted at random, which he had had the ill-fortune of being subjected to on more than a dozen occasions. He calmly obliged, and the policeman went about his business. His legs trembled as the policeman ran his hands over him. The huge hands went up Uhuru's legs, lingered for what appeared like eternity around his crotch before proceeding to his torso. Uhuru had quite some experience of personal humiliation but he was still yet to develop immunity to this degradation that he had to endure now and again.

"Any weapons, boy?"

"No, sir." Uhuru smiled affably at the policeman. One had to appear relaxed and cooperative. That was the rule of the game.

"A machete perhaps?" The policeman grinned with malice.

"Machete?" Uhuru was bewildered that anyone could possibly conceal such a tool on his person.

The policeman laughed sarcastically. "Don't know what a machete is, boy? The weapon of choice in Africa, isn't it?" Uhuru said nothing. Cars hooted in the distance.

"Cocaine smuggling like the troublesome Antilleans, eh?" the policeman persisted in his interrogation.

"No, sir." Uhuru stayed calm in face of this adversity. When talking to the law and order men, one had to keep answers short. This was a survival instinct that each immigrant acquired over time. Getting verbose had the danger of one venturing into some indelicate word exchange with a potential to send tempers flaring. And in such an eventuality, it was very clear which of the two the courts would believe. Thus, Uhuru remained composed and polite to the letter. As the body search was in progress, Uhuru noticed that a little crowd had formed to witness his broad daylight humiliation. And they were quite a curious lot of all shades of humanity's colors; from the dark of skin as dense as the blackout that engulfed Rotterdam following the Second World War bombing to the very white of a pale mask of death. But Uhuru knew he would disappoint their curiosity. He had no concealed weapons or illicit drugs. In fact, he had never handled a weapon and despised the men and women of violence. There were many of those back home.

"Okay, boy. Have a good day and make sure to keep out of trouble," the policeman barked. Disappointed at not seeing handcuffs fastened on him, the curious sea of faces melted in the midmorning Rotterdam crowd.

"Good day, sir." Uhuru pulled himself together and resumed his stride, albeit a little bit uneasy. Of this encounter he would tell none among his circle of acquaintances since it did happen to most of them with the predictable regularity and singular monotony of the chiming bells of medieval St. Laurentius church, a few blocks from where he now walked.

———

Uhuru let himself into the apartment slowly. He wasn't sure if his two roommates were still sleeping, and he didn't want to wake them up. Pierre simply adored lying in. If left to his own devices, Pierre would happily not move out of bed, deriving much pleasure in the remote control at his command, restlessly going through all the channels on his 30-inch Philips flat screen. Greg had been out partying for most of the night, as he was apt to do on any given Friday evening. When Uhuru entered the living room, he found Pierre comfortably lying on the brown leather sofa, bought from Winkel van Sinkel, the secondhand store. Indeed, most furniture in their apartment was purchased from Winkel van Sinkel. Each of the men had his own bedroom in the apartment, sharing the other utilities. And it was obvious the occupants of this apartment cared not a straw about furniture and interior design but were big on electronic gadgetry. A stereo installation with powerful loudspeakers and another 30-inch television set took up much of the living room. There were plastic flowers in a plastic vase on a glass coffee table. And the understanding among them was that they cooked and cleaned dishes in turn. No specific arrangements were made about cleaning the house with the result that the living room and kitchen were almost always a sore to the eye. Once Pierre's underpants had hang on the back of a chair for weeks, purportedly drying. There were dirty plates that were occasionally retrieved from under the sofa where they hadn't been missed for days.

When Uhuru entered the living room, Pierre grumbled that his heavy steps had woken him from his nap. Indeed, after a breakfast of tea (with plenty of sugar), toast, jam, boiled egg, and a cigar, he had lain in the sofa, savoring the idleness of a Saturday morning, free from the dreary daily chore of sorting post.

"Thought I had slipped in as quietly as a snake." Uhuru pulled at the Velcro hook and loop flaps of his green windbreaker, opening the jacket. Green wasn't his color but there hadn't been windbreakers in orange or blue, his favorite colors, at the Wibra summer sale two years ago. He shrugged his sturdy body out of the jacket and tossed it carelessly on the dining table.

"Next time round you had better try to be more discrete, my friend." Pierre stretched his arms and suppressed a yawn. Pierre was short and spare but with the energy of a stubborn mule. He had an oblong-shaped head, like an ostrich's egg.

"Exactly what I did, dude. Closed the door gently behind me and tiptoed." Uhuru spoke pleasantly, pulled a chair from the table, and sat down to face Pierre.

"That might be so but you didn't have it all well managed."

"How do you mean?"

"I heard the key as you opened the apartment door. You would make a lousy James Bond, dude." Pierre pointed his fingers at Uhuru in a shooting gesture.

"Talking of James Bond, are we renting a video for the weekend? Greg spoke highly of Quentin Tarantino's *Kill Bill*. What about that?"

"You don't mean to suggest you have forgotten tonight's party? Greg's ex-colleagues are coming over, remember?"

Noticing for the first time a copy of *Rotterdam Weekly Herald* lying on the carpet next to Pierre, Uhuru inquired, "What does the paper say?"

"Same tired recycled stuff. It is all about immigrants, and immigrants, and immigrants. Makes me sick to the bone." Pierre picked up the newspaper.

"Surely there are more interesting things beyond the front page," Uhuru said. He, too, was tired of those screaming headlines that vilified people like him. Verbal lynching he called it.

"Scandals and the like. Interesting stuff if you seek intellectual challenge in that kind of trite. Certainly not my cup of tea! Why should I make it my business to know if a particular politician is gay and has been doing booming business with male prostitutes in a public park? Oh, I don't give a shit if one of our straight-laced mayors is a habitual surfer of Internet pornographic sites." And after a pause, "Such pieces of stale information eat away at my intellectual foundation. If it weren't for the lack of money, I would subscribe to the *NRC* or the *Groene Amsterdammer*." Pierre half rose in the sofa and puffed luxuriously at his cigarette before declaring, "Well, we need to do some shopping for tonight's party ... and this darned place needs some tidying up." And as an afterthought, he inquired if Uhuru had managed to buy the book.

"No."

"Disappointed?" Pierre threw the newspaper on the floor and stretched to his full length on the sofa.

"Not at all." Anyway, Uhuru hadn't felt so hopeful to begin with. There was a part of him that had never believed much in that book. Nonetheless, he had gone in search of Johannes de Lange's book, partly out of desperation and partly to please Greg, his landlord.

———

Greg's ex-colleagues at Jansen & van Amersfoort were expected that Saturday evening. And Greg had made much fuss about the fact that some of them were white, showing, perhaps, that he was well-integrated into Dutch society. Uhuru had yet to socialize with white people outside the work environment. He was excited to get in touch with the true Dutch natives, for up till this point, he might as well have been living in the heartland of Africa. Uhuru had set up his mind to engage the true Dutch natives in an intellectual discussion of equals. He looked forward to discussing Dutch poets, artists, and philosophers. Uhuru had read much about Hugo de Groot, Christiaan Huygens, Antoni van Leeuwenhoek, and other famous Dutch statesmen, scientists, and philosophers of past centuries. How he would have loved to show off his knowledge to the natives, a group that would surely understand the significance of these great scholars!

But when Greg's friends, a rowdy, carefree crowd, arrived that evening, it was immediately apparent that they were recent immigrants from the Balkans, and that Uhuru had a better command of the Dutch language. Nonetheless, their gaiety and easy manner made up for Uhuru's disappointment. Whiffs of expensive perfume from sensual feminine bodies, sweating masculine odors, and the lingering smell of tobacco hovered over the crowded room. Washington Keya stood in a corner surrounded by a group of Africans attentively listening to his theories on good governance in Africa. Washington Keya had a commanding presence, and it wasn't at all puzzling that he had earned his way into exile after vigorously supporting a group of young army officers to stage a military coup, which was, unfortunately, mercilessly crushed. It was rumored that had the coup succeeded, he would have become yet another authoritarian African president determined to rule for life, presiding over vast gold, diamond, and oil mines. In another corner of the room, one of the ex-Yugoslavian men shared a marijuana joint with Amadu, an African poet, but now unemployed of Amsterdam southeast. He always grumbled that immigrants, legal or illegal (he insisted the distinction was purely academic), were callously balkanized into pockets of desperation and depravity and condemned to a state of eternal humiliation by nation states eager to wrongly explain away their failures on some powerless but visible foe. Nobody took his concerns seriously, and Uhuru supposed the white men attentively listening to a recitation of one of his powerfully moving poems would equally dismiss his views.

"Just like us," Uhuru said to Alisi, a slender, half-Asian and half-African beauty queen with intelligent, slightly slanting eyes. She wore a bright red, backless mini dress that accentuated her soft curves and exaggerated the size of her firm breasts, casting her in a beauty that was hard to find in the Northern Hemisphere pedigree. Alisi's desirable dress made Uhuru in his colorful Mandela shirt and cheap jean trousers feel positively anachronistic. His only saving grace, he reflected, were his trendy shoes; van Bommel shoes in dark brown suede. Alisi was Greg's girlfriend of the last five months, and on this particular evening, she did awaken in Uhuru a longing for Mapenzi that he determinedly suppressed. They were in the kitchen cleaning up and mixing drinks for the guests. The kitchen was a narrow room with bare amenities. There wasn't much beyond the gas cooker and refrigerator, and it was hard to imagine how one could perform a simple task like boiling an egg. But the austerity of the kitchen was no impediment to good cooking, as Alisi, on countless occasions, had ably demonstrated.

"They laugh a lot and are quite reasonable," Alisi said. She passed on a glass to Uhuru to dry. "And their first question to you is not, 'when are you going back to your country?' You know how that one demoralizes me. It clearly summarizes the native's affinity for the foreigner!"

Uhuru's face lit up in an intellectual glow. "I guess these folks don't have to ask such questions. It is shared destiny, Alisi. They and we have a shared destiny of hopelessness. We are all refugees struggling to define for ourselves a new niche in a rather hostile melee. I think I know why they are quite different from all other Europeans." Indeed, Uhuru sensed a kind of kindred feeling with the ex-Yugoslavs, the same feeling of belonging he experienced when strolling along Colonel Pokoto Street, the fear of getting mugged by street robbers notwithstanding. In Rotterdam he felt as if it was required of him to apologize to the natives for the very air that he breathed and for each step he made.

"Why do you think they are unlike other Europeans?" Alisi washed her hands. She had finished with this round of washing plates, glasses, and cutlery.

"They are poor. And just like we folks from Africa, they do not know how to live in peace with each other. It is the weakness of the extrovert, believe you me."

Alisi said she didn't quite follow the reasoning. Uhuru wanted to expound on his hypothesis but there wasn't time enough. Greg burst into the kitchen and declared there was total drought in the living room.

"Alisi, some brandy for my mate, Slavoljub," Greg said urgently. "Now that is one great guy … a boner and slicer of the old school." Slavoljub drank nothing but brandy, bottles of which had been bought cheaply from a discount store just over the German border where Greg and Alisi shopped once a month.

There was another affable ex-Yugoslav, Goran, who drank like a fish and swore at every swig of the bottle. Even Pierre, reputed for his ability to hold alcohol rather well, was no match to the gregarious Goran. It seemed that at any one time his hands were either holding a bottle of whisky or busy pinching a provocative bottom of one of the African women. Goran had taken particular interest in Latasha, a young African lady of stunning beauty. When the DJ, Pierre, decided time was ripe to do some serious dancing, he chose a dazzling bass display of loud *soukous* music that dispersed the depressing solitude of a spring whose grayness was indistinguishable from the griminess of winter.

"Now, folks!" Pierre shouted, repeatedly throwing hands into the air as if he was the famous DJ XjeT of Radio 3 fame. "Time to loosen up and show this damned cold place how we are determined to enjoy our lives."

The music blazed from a 120 Watt 3 Way Reflex System, shaking the room and energizing the guests and their hosts. Goran took on Latasha (she had been a dancer with Wenge

Musica before pitching tent in the Netherlands where she had unsuccessfully tried her hand at pole-dancing in a dingy Amsterdam adult club), and the way those two whirled and twisted left everyone bewildered. There was no mistake. Latasha had smote Goran, and the evidence was there for all and sundry that he wanted much more than forcing stiff hips to respond to psychedelic *soukous* music. Now Latasha's lacquered nails were digging into the back of Goran's neck, and he returned the suggestive gesture of intimacy by clasping his hands tight on her generous bottom.

Greg whispered ecstatically to Uhuru. "That lecherous bastard is going to screw Latasha, I swear."

"You don't mind, do you?" Uhuru lit a cigarette. It was his fourteenth that Saturday. Although he had moral objections about indiscriminate one-night stands, he saw no reason why Goran shouldn't lay Latasha since she was unspoken for. He imagined that given Goran's liberties with Latasha, he had to be free and single.

"She has such a cute ass. I've always wanted to lay her," Greg said with jealousy. "And by Jove! one day …"

Uhuru tried to raise his voice above the din. "Come on Greg! You've got Alisi, and she is a stunning beauty. You've got an eye for beauty, man." Uhuru was unlike Greg or Pierre who drew enormous pleasure flirting with women. Over the years, he had hardened himself against thinking of the pleasures of the flesh. For he realized that obsession with such matters might tempt him to betray Mapenzi, the one woman he so loved.

Greg ignored the compliment. "By the way, where is my Alisi?"

"In the kitchen. She is preparing some snacks."

Just then Alisi appeared in the kitchen doorway carrying a tray full of one of her delicious recipes—red pepper seasoned meatballs that had to be dipped in chili sauce. Uhuru simply adored those meatballs and was so glad Alisi had offered her services. The last time the three men had organized a party, Pierre had insisted, against better advice from Greg and Uhuru, on spending money on a variety of cheeses. The cheese was hardly touched because guests and hosts alike found the taste too atrocious for palates more used to delicacies such as fried grasshoppers and flying ants.

Alisi picked her way slowly through the crowd of partygoers, offering the guests a taste of her good cooking. And there was unanimity, as borne by the generous compliments and cries of sincere delight of the mostly beer-drinking crowd, that the meatballs were a divine treat and an elaborate bite. Presently, Alisi reached Greg and Uhuru. In fact, it had been clear to Uhuru right from the time that she appeared in the doorway, her focus was Greg, and one false step from Greg could result in a fight. There were frequent quarrels between the two. Often the rows got so bad that they didn't speak to each other for days on end. But their mutual need for each other was so overpowering, and they found themselves drawn together again.

Alisi admonished Greg for not helping out in the kitchen.

"You haven't done a single thing. Just sauntering about and waiting to be served like an Ashanti King. Aren't you a typical African man with a village headman's mentality? Uhuru has done his bit, and so has Pierre, in between playing the music."

Truth was that Pierre had entered the kitchen only once to deposit shards of a broken glass in the green, biodegradable garbage bin.

"Now, now, darling! We all possibly can't cram in that kitchen. Before you continue accusing me, it would be very well to remember that someone has got to entertain the visitors and that demanding task happens to be on the shoulders of Greg Okafor, your sweetheart."

Alisi forced the tray into Greg's hands. "Very convenient, indeed! I, too, need some fun. I am going to dance with that pal of yours, Slavoljub."

"See that blonde Serbian sitting on his lap?" Greg asked. Displaying a broad mischievous smile, he smacked Alisi rather fondly on the bottom while delicately holding on to the tray with the other hand. And that indulgent whack seemed to do the trick, seducing Alisi into a state of calmness, restoring the peace between them. "That is his lady, and she is likely not to get amused sitting idle while her man is snatched from her laps by some Afro-Asian belle. But I dare say give it a shot." And the white lady was a heavyset blonde with an expressionless face. She was built like a weightlifter on anabolic steroids, an anti-aphrodisiac Babushka.

Alisi cast a brief but reverent look at the blonde. Her implacable attitude, which was spoiling for a fight with Greg, slowly, but irreversibly, gave way to a radiant smile of extraordinary charm. "Come, Uhuru, let's dance."

Uhuru stared meekly at Greg who nodded his encouragement. Then as Alisi pulled a timid Uhuru by the scruff of his collar, Greg laughed heartily and sauntered off with the tray to serve the guests.

The party was already a success, and Uhuru was beginning to enjoy himself. Whoever said that living in the anonymity of illegality did not have its own thrilling moments of happiness? Beaming inside with contentment, dazzled by the serenity of the music and the celebratory air of human pleasure, as can only be generated on a festive evening, Uhuru entirely forgot his clandestine existence and felt one with the crowd of revelers. As far as he could see, everyone had managed to get into party mood. He saw Milagros Gonzalez, an immigrant from the Dominican Republic, working as a KLM stewardess. Milagros was Alisi's friend. She had returned from Miami that morning.

Milagros was talking to a man Uhuru didn't immediately recognize, and they seemed to have warmed up to each other's company. *Perhaps a friend of Pierre or Greg*, he thought. Maybe he was her boyfriend, although he didn't quite remember if Milagros had found a new boyfriend. She had broken up with her last boyfriend, some Dutch computer nerd eight years her junior. She said he was rather childish, which given his twenty-two years didn't surprise Uhuru at all.

Uhuru and Alisi joined the others on the floor, dancing to another fast *soukous* beat. As Uhuru moved backwards to avoid Alisi's heaving thrusts crushing into him, he bumped into a massive body floating on an ocean of blaring saxophones, ecstatic guitar, captivating drums, and the seductive singing of Orchestra Savannah Juju's lead singer.

"Mind your step!" Goran boomed with laughter.

"Sorry!" Uhuru apologized. "Not enough room in here."

"What is important is that we are having fun, not so Latasha?" Goran shouted. But Latasha was taking the entire dancing business rather seriously and was oblivious to her dancing partner's remarks.

"Name is Goran." He extended a big hairy hand to Uhuru.

He must be quite drunk, decided Uhuru. They had been introduced earlier. Well, Uhuru reflected, if Goran wanted another handshake he would not deny it. So they shook hands. Later, when the music had stopped and Latasha had gone to the bathroom to "powder her face," Goran sought Uhuru out. He said it was so warm inside and perhaps they would go to the balcony for fresh air and a chat. Uhuru wasn't so sure about what he might have in common with Goran. He had heard from Greg that he had been a pharmacist before the civil war in the Balkans that had cost the lives of his wife and two-year old daughter. He had tried to overcome his loss and now worked for a road construction firm, operating an excavator. They stepped out onto the crowded balcony. In the distance one could see the lights on the Erasmus Bridge and the headlamps of cars racing over the bridge. A dog barked, there was a swish of tires on the wet highway (there was a light drizzle), and the sound of merriment back in the living room seemed to have taken on a new congenial intensity. It had been an exceptionally cold night for the end of March but the chilly freshness of the balcony was a welcome change from the warm and stuffy living room.

Goran wished to know more about Africa, and his interest momentarily hinged on the magical allure of the music. He said he simply adored the last song.

"I say," Goran said appreciatively, "that was a master piece!"

"Yeah," Uhuru agreed.

"What was the chap singing about? Love, I presume?"

"I don't understand the language. But Latasha once told me it is about a businessman in Kinshasa, a diamond dealer."

"The song is about diamonds, then? Like Paul Simon's *Diamonds on the Soles of Her Shoes*?"

"Not quite. The musician is praising the businessman for his philanthropic work but also stressing he is the sexiest and most desirable man on the entire African continent. If you have enough money, two hundred euro, you can solicit the talents of our musicians to sing your praise to the high heavens. We call it *dedication.* You might be at a loss identifying with all the virtuous qualities that they would ascribe to your personage. Most chaps know these are platitudes but, nonetheless, they enjoy every bit of the praise since it makes them experience a bit of immortal infallibility, like our own leaders back home."

"You folks have an intriguing culture," Goran declared, with a puzzled frown on the face. He seemed rather disappointed that the melodious song was not mostly about love. Now he wanted to know from Uhuru how African women were like in bed. Uhuru being a man accustomed to living with the accusation of unnecessary moral correctness was totally unprepared for such vulgarity. At a loss as to how best to proceed in the company of a man decidedly eager to explore a new territory of sensual delight, Uhuru mumbled something about inexperience in such delicate matters.

Goran started to laugh. "You aren't women shy, are you?" He was unaware of Uhuru's excruciating discomfort.

"I am a married man," Uhuru said, as his thoughts carried him to the other end of the globe, overwhelming his sense of loneliness. Then he told Goran about Mapenzi and how his devotion to her could not be adequately captured by human vocabulary. Uhuru's eyes sparkled with love and sheer fondness. He labored on, stressing that it was for Mapenzi's good and the good of their daughter that he had made the decision to come to the Netherlands in the hope of finding meaningful employment. "I haven't seen her in six and a half years, and during that time, I have not betrayed her trust."

Uhuru had never cheated on his wife. When Pierre, and occasionally Greg, went off to "release themselves," he considered it immoral to accompany them to the prostitutes in one of the popular streets. The last time when Pierre was off to an address not far from their apartment, he had said, "You must come one day. There is nothing to be shy about. Every self-respecting Dutchman, even your average respectable politician, considers it a matter of honor and pride to use the services of a whore. Ever stopped to consider why prostitution has been legalized in this country?" At this, Uhuru had shot back saying that just because one politician's sexual exploits and subsequent peccadilloes in an Amsterdam brothel had been the subject of focused interest, it didn't mean that one should generalize about Dutch politicians.

Goran whistled with undisguised respect. "Can't believe my ears, man! You haven't laid a woman in as many years!"

Uhuru gave a little embarrassed smile of acquiescence, and he would have found an excuse and left. But what counted now was that he had finally, after many years in the Netherlands, got into casual conversation with a white man. It didn't matter that he was not Dutch but ex-Yugoslavian. He was probably a Serb or Croat or Muslim. What did it matter? In spite of his fixation on African women and his painfully candid manner of speech, Uhuru decided that Goran was rather entertaining. Uhuru's shyness discussing the sexuality of African women led him to ask Goran rather abruptly, "Have you also worked at Jansen & van Amersfoort?" Greg's constant praise of his former profession had conditioned Uhuru to believe that all his friends and acquaintances were men and women that were directly or indirectly associated with abattoirs.

Goran gave a hearty laugh, before saying pleasantly, "Two days and that was more than enough! There was this overpowering stench that clung on my skin and got on my nerves. I admire Slavoljub and all those blokes. How they managed to put up with that place is beyond my Slavic ken! And what do you do my friend?"

"This and that … not much really. However, much of it is of a temporary nature … very temporary and without a prospect for a prosperous future and quiet retirement."

"I must admit it sounds as dreary and forbidding as the apocalypse!" Goran enthused, laughing. "But what is it exactly? You don't look a boner and slicer to me."

"Well, cleaning jobs like most folks in the neighborhood. I mostly do the restaurant circuit but there is the occasional factory. I have also had a stint picking strawberries and digging up asparagus. That way I have been running from the economic recession. But, aha, one can't quite hide from it." Uhuru shrugged his shoulders and felt in his trouser pocket. He presently removed a lighter. Then he put a hand in his shirt pocket. Failing to find a cigarette and observing that he hadn't seen Goran smoking, he proceeded, "The blooming recession has now caught up with me. Three weeks of unemployment for one not entitled to any benefits is too long a period. Mind you, not that I would accept handouts!" To a degree this was true of Uhuru. Even if he had been entitled to unemployment benefits, he would have been at pains to accept the generosity of society. He had been brought to celebrate the dignity of hard work as a way of earning one's daily potato. Social benefits, he felt, should be reserved for people that could not participate actively on the labor force for reasons of infirmity. In this, as in matters of matrimonial honor, Uhuru was truly conservative. He believed that it was the man's divine duty to earn the family's daily potato. So had it been in his family, and so would it always be. He intended to carry that responsibility as a badge of honor and would consider any form of work as long as it would enable him fend for his wife and daughter. "At this stage, I am desperate for employment. I would willingly jump at anything under this gray sky. Cleaning rooms in nursing homes or changing soiled linens. One at my age needs to be active, otherwise the idleness of underemployment tempts one to experiment on dangerous ventures. You know the devil shows his abundant generosity to idle hands." Uhuru smiled slowly. Goran seemed to have sobered up, for he listened attentively without interrupting. All the while Uhuru felt Goran's eyes intensely studying his face under the soft glare of the yellow balcony lamp.

Uhuru's spontaneity and warmth must have mellowed Goran's senses, leading him to a magnanimous spontaneity, "I wish I was in a position of some authority and advantage to offer you a job, my African friend. Has anybody ever told you that your strict brand of faithfulness to a wife you haven't seen in more than six years is commendable? You are so unlike many unimaginative, complaining, and lazy men who would jump at the first opportunity to down tools in exchange for an easy comfy ride on the social benefits train."

"Thank you for the kind words," Uhuru muttered.

Thus, moved and impressed, Goran extracted a wallet from his trouser pocket and removed a crumpled piece of paper. It was a newspaper cutting that he gave to Uhuru. The shabbiness of the paper belied the significance of the advertisement, and even at closer scrutiny, did not reveal that it would profoundly chart Uhuru's entire future and become a subject of hushed and pained discussions for a long time to come.

"I was saving that for a friend in Utrecht. We hail from the same town. He worked as a baker before the war—his was easily the best *pogacha* bread in the entire Yugoslavia. Being a man good at languages, he quickly picked up the Dutch language and managed to find work up north in a refugee camp as an interpreter. But jobs of that nature, however comfortable and well paying, do not last long. He was again on the streets, and has been ever since. "

Uhuru studied the piece of paper, an advertisement for a job as a gardener for a mansion in the posh Kralingen neighborhood of Rotterdam. His face lit up with relief, for he felt deep inside that this was his next job, and an easy one to perform. He visualized himself in overalls mowing and weeding, watering plants (magnolias and azaleas at this time in spring, he imagined), and sweeping away fallen leaves. His excitement was such that he could have kissed Goran were it not for the social unacceptability of such a familiar gesture or he could have thrown his arms around the ex-Yugoslav lifting him up in a display of exuberant appreciation had it not been for the man's bulky size.

"Thanks, dude." Uhuru was truly touched. In the last three weeks of joblessness and worrying about his future and the well-being of his wife and daughter, he had quite forgotten the magnanimity of man. All that he saw was a hostile world in which a few privileged by right of birth lorded over the disadvantaged, a class in overwhelming majority and to which he was an unfortunate representative.

"You don't need to thank me, dude. I am just doing my bit for another soul. As you have read they are looking for a gardener with years of experience. Have you done any gardening before?"

"Long, long time ago." Uhuru remembered the many years ago when he was growing up in the backwaters of the Uganda countryside. With his mother and four siblings they would rise up very early before sunrise. In single file they would head for the fields to do a spot of gardening, hoeing the parched, red earth before the children washed, eating a quick breakfast of roasted cassava which was washed down with a mug of lukewarm black tea, and jogging to school. The school, St. John Bosco Primary School that was run by dedicated Dutch missionaries, was an odd seven kilometers from their home.

"Then you will need to draw on that experience," Goran said thoughtfully.

"I do have lots of knowledge about rocks, though. I studied Siberian rocks at university." Uhuru glowed with pride. He now supposed that the solidity of his university study uniquely placed him at an advantage to get a gardener's job.

"Siberian rocks!" Goran thundered in utter merriment. Laughing uncontrollably, he shouted some rapid words in a language Uhuru supposed must have been Serbian. Slavoljub and another of his countryman joined them on the balcony, laughing even louder than Goran.

Slavoljub struggled to suppress peals of laughter. "I say, my good fellow, why the devil did you have to study Siberian rocks?"

"He could have done carpentry." Uhuru hadn't seen Amadu join them on the balcony. "How often have I told you that Uhuru? Siberian rocks, my foot!" the African poet said with condescending gravity.

Surrounded by amused faces Uhuru could think of no more to say than join in the laughter. Oftentimes, Uhuru asked himself that very question as well. But he knew the answer. There had been a university scholarship from a generous foreign government offered to a bright and promising Ugandan student to major in Siberian rocks. Then a government minister hailing from Uhuru's home village had lobbied the people at the education ministry, leading them to select Uhuru for the scholarship. It was a festive moment, a great celebration of academic achievement, and the entire village was invited to a party sending off one of their own abroad. But amidst all the colorful political speeches that were awash that day, Uhuru had his own misgivings about Siberian rocks. There was the reality of finding suitable employment once back home after completion of his studies. Yes, he also doubted if his studies were relevant when it came to dealing with the enormous economic and political challenges facing his country and indeed the entire continent. He did acutely realize, right at the very outset, that solving Africa's enormous problems did not depend on waiting for clever solutions from a mind educated in matters related to Siberian rocks.

Chapter 3 Meeting the employer

The requisite call had been made and a telephone interview, which appeared more like twelve minutes of harsh and merciless interrogation, had taken place between the job seeker and prospective employer, a woman with a commanding voice that resonated with prosperity and firm authority. She had identified herself as Inge Baleman-Ruyter. She didn't inquire about Uhuru's country of birth, even though his staccato Dutch betrayed that he was not a native of this land of polders and windmills. The lady was keen on exploring Uhuru's skills, insisting that if the ad had been clear about one thing then it was the desire to employ an experienced gardener, nothing less and nothing more.

"Did you read and comprehend the advertisement?" Inge pressed on, mercilessly.

"Yes, mum." Uhuru was fearful that Inge might disconnect the line anytime.

"I don't want some inexperienced fellow walking about my garden and killing off the plants! If you have never done this work before say so and not waste my time."

Uhuru saw his fortunes sinking and his hopes whittling to despair. He had to salvage himself, and quick. Oftentimes when he mentioned to prospective employers about his academic qualifications they tended to respond in a standard way: too qualified for the simple and dirty tasks on offer, and they immediately lost interest. He didn't understand why they responded so. After all he just wanted to work, and he had provided an honest answer about his education. Amadu had said that he should never volunteer information about his education, since it tended to make the prospective employers rather uneasy. They disliked, said Amadu, immigrants with brains. But now here he was, talking to this lady that held the key to his next job. What should he do? Shouldn't he tell her everything in the hope that she might find his wealth of theoretical knowledge on Siberian rocks an added advantage? But what if she found such training superfluous and a total mismatch for the vacancy at hand? He realized that his aspirations and indeed his entire future depended on the choice of words he would use in marketing his university training. Too much praise could be catastrophic and so would a failure to adequately highlight his expertise on Siberian rocks. So he decided to gamble. Inge had listened to his enthusiastic recital of his qualifications, and why he thought he was the best-suited candidate for the gardener job. And finally in a tone of voice that was at once encouraging and aloof she had agreed to schedule a face-to-face interview with Uhuru. He was mightily relieved that he wasn't required to write an application letter. The Royal Chelloil experience had left him traumatized and suspicious of application letters. Amadu, the poet, had once recounted his experience with application letters, and what he had said had cemented Uhuru's distrust of sending letters as a means to secure a job. Amadu had sent in an application letter, but after waiting for close to four weeks without a courtesy of an answer, he had decided to follow-up with an email inquiry about the status of his application. There was no answer forthcoming. He sent a second email which elicited a response, albeit of a disconcerting nature. Amadu was warned that his practice of making innumerable unsolicited inquiries would forthwith not be tolerated. He had overstepped the boundaries of accepted civilized communication, the response email emphasized, and persistence in this practice risked him being classified as a stalker or crack pot, and the law was unlikely to take kindly of this sort of misfits who were best home in a psychiatric institution. Deflated and defenseless to prove that he wasn't any of these nasty things but a desperate and upright alien seeking honest employment, Amadu had broken down and wept. Few believed the tale, but Uhuru was among those that didn't doubt the sincerity of Amadu's humiliating ordeal.

Now the prospect of going to the exclusivity and comfort of a grand mansion in Kralingen on Thursday of that week brought a certain apprehension to one such as him, used as he was to the smell of the decaying dampness of poverty that seemed to define Uhuru's Rotterdam neighborhood. Amadu took a witty poetical stance to this deprivation, assuring Uhuru that theirs was the only place in the entire land where cockroaches and rare mice species had taken refuge, a matter to be proud of in the untiring global quest of preserving endangered species.

"Get yourself some decent clothes, Uhuru," Amadu advised as they sat in apartment number 741 E in Prof. A.S. van Vredeman, going over the events of the last weekend's party with the ex-Yugoslavs and the team of enthusiastic African and spirited Caribbean party goers. "Don't let yourself be denied the job because you wore tasteless clothes. Never mind that this is one of those 3-d jobs ... dirty, dangerous, and degrading ... you should be dressed to the nines for any job interview."

"My Mandela shirt will do." Uhuru was overflowing with confidence.

"Suppose lady-what-is-her-name can't stand Mandela? What then?"

"Why should anybody dislike the old man?"

"Margaret Thatcher lashed at him with her handbag, berating the poor soul for being the leader of a typical terrorist organization."

"What do you suggest, then?"

"If I were you, I would definitely settle for something more neutral."

———

That afternoon Uhuru was in city center, looking for a bargain. New clothes, he had decided, after that chat with Amadu. There was a sale going at Erasmus & Brug but the prices, despite a twenty-percent discount, were way out of his reach. He passed the Versace store, eyeing the window display with unrepentant envy, and he winced at the Hugo Boss store prices. Uhuru finally found himself standing in front of the city's leading fashion outlet, House of Piet Snygrens, by Royal Appointment since 1887. He was somehow reminded of Colonel Pokoto Street. Watoto Inc. the specialists in children's wear since 1972. He contemplated the difference between the two stores, and he was particularly jolted at discovering the recency of Watoto Inc., in comparison to House of Piet Snygrens, an establishment of solid historical roots. What was experience beginning in 1972, in comparison to a treasured tradition whose seal of royal approval spanned over a century? A large board advertised that all items were being offered at a sixty percent discount. The offer was related, proclaimed the board, to reasons of restructuring the store's interior. It was Uhuru's opportunity to make a cheap purchase of an expensive brand name. Into the store he marched, joining the multitude of treasure hunters.

He had hardly been a minute in the exclusive store when he made a disconcerting observation. One of the shop assistants, a pale anorexic looking woman, probably in her mid-twenties, was trailing behind him. Uhuru went from one rack to another, and so did the eyes of the shop assistant. Well, shop assistants that followed hot on Uhuru's heels were not an entirely new phenomenon, frustrating and humiliating as that experience was bound to be. There was none among his circle of acquaintances whose conspicuousness in shops had not been carefully watched under a gaze of contempt and intense suspicion. Uhuru would have liked to shout at the woman, "Mind your business, lady! I am not about to take shoppers hostage and rob the damn place." Out of the corner of his eye he stole a glance at her. She appeared like on the verge of hysteria each time Uhuru's hand examined a shirt on the rack. Then Uhuru paced up and down, like the other shoppers. From the shirts section he relocated to the trousers. All along the young lady's shadow hung over him like Damocles' sword so eager to strike. She would occasionally remove this or that garment and pretend to wipe off some unseen dirt from a trouser or scarf but all the while never losing sight of her quarry. Uhuru pulled down a trouser from the shelf and held it against his Mandela shirt. He surreptitiously looked at the shop assistant. This time round she looked to be gearing up to utter a scream that would no doubt descend on the police station, half a kilometer or so down the street, in a deafening roar of an intensity enough to rattle the cups and spill the coffee in the neighboring restaurant. Uhuru made great effort to behave as if he was oblivious of the woman's shadowing figure. All the fellows that had lived here longer than him advised this was the best approach to adapt under circumstances of intense surveillance. "Remain composed and unruffled and that way, your self-esteem does not disintegrate," Amadu had once counseled Greg who not able to entertain this behavior anymore had shouted rudely at a shop assistant. The police had been called in, and he was lucky he hadn't been thrown into the cooler.

"Are you looking for anything in particular?" the woman asked with deliberate mocking commiseration. To Uhuru the woman sounded like the perfect inquisitor.

He stopped examining a beige Dockers trouser and put his hands in his trouser pockets, a neutral unthreatening posture, according to the wise counsel of Amadu, that self-styled rational existentialist.

"Looking for a Dockers trouser, but I seem to have found what I want," Uhuru said, as decently as he could muster. Uhuru had been forced to make up his mind, and for his interview he would dress in the beige Dockers trouser and a light blue shirt that he had picked up the previous summer from a sale at V&D. That appearance, he hoped, would satisfy Inge Baleman-Ruyter.

"Okay," the shop assistant declared. "Now if you will follow me ... payment is at the counter, sir. That one has a seventy-percent discount but you might still find it expensive." Her tone was maddeningly contemptuous, and the sneer on her lips diabolically humiliating.

And when they reached the counter she inquired, "Cash or debit card?"

Of course as an illegal inhabitant of the Netherlands there was no way any bank would have allowed him to open an account. One needed a Social Fiscal Number to access any social services, and such a number could only be obtained from the Tax Office. Of course Uhuru knew of some diehard illegal aliens who had somehow managed to lay their hands on Social Fiscal Numbers. Uhuru had decidedly refrained from exploring ways of following their gallantry believing it was a crime greater than being in the country illegally. He wasn't a criminal, as far as he could see. He was only a man looking for a better opportunity in order to fend for those under his charge.

With a redeeming smile Uhuru handed thirty euro to the shop assistant. Because he was so desperate to show that he was a reasonable decent fellow without diabolic motives, he wanted to ask her to keep the change. But he knew this wasn't an accepted practice and one that might earn him more scorn than acceptance from this woman. Besides, he reflected, he had better save the small change for an eventual present for Juliana. He very much wanted to buy for her the lovely brown bear that he had seen in the toy store. When the woman handed him the plastic carrier bag Uhuru said, "Good day, madam." He hoped that this display of gentlemanly behavior and articulation of civil sentiment might be enough demonstration to this pathetic woman that ethnic minorities were not by definition a batch of uncouth criminals.

—

As Uhuru walked out of the elegance of House of Piet Snygrens and joined the multitudes in the wide Rotterdam street, the idea that most of his unwilling hosts considered him of dubious character caused him to falter a step or two. But he bravely forged ahead, plastic carrier bag with the respectable logo of House of Piet Snygrens in his firm grip. He realized it would be no good for his self-esteem to crumble in face of ignorant bigotry. *To survive in this prejudicial environment*, thought Uhuru, as he climbed onto a crowded tram, *one needs a lion's courage to shoulder the subtle hostility.*

Twenty-five minutes later he was sitting in the coolness of a Turkish teahouse in Blaak with Amadu and Ibrahim Sani, a man perpetually excited at trying out anything new, however impractical and improbable. This time round, amidst wild gesticulations, he was briefing Amadu and Uhuru about a business plan he was working on with a couple of other dubious fellows. The scheme, he swore, was sure to earn them lots of money without even bothering to invest a single penny, or more incredulously, time. Last time Uhuru had met him, he had gone on for hours on end about how he and his mates were going to collect all the half smoked cigarettes littering the streets of Rotterdam. The idea was basically simple: scoop out the tobacco and roll it into new cigarettes that would be marketed under their own unique brand name, Cigara Afrikaland, with the fitting slogan, *The cool smoke that cleans your environment.* Ibrahim Sani and his mates had indeed gone about collecting half smoked cigarettes from the streets of Rotterdam. They gave up the enterprise after one week when harsh reality dawned, and they realized it would just never work. There were many that laughed at this futile undertaking, and Pierre was heard to comment, "In any case the outcome would have been more disastrous had the poor devil fixed his mind on entering the contraband cigarettes business. Good he heeded my counsel not to tread that dangerous path."

Now Ibrahim Sani suddenly remembered that he had to meet an associate in this new business venture and would not wait for the tea that was taking such a long time to come.

"Time is money," Ibrahim Sani declared in a sagely tone. He rose and left in a hurry.

Amadu and Uhuru waited for their tea, delighting in a piano composition by the eclectic Ilhan Usmanbaş that played soothingly in the background. When they parted ways, Uhuru headed straight for the public library where he spent almost four hours poring over books on gardening as part of his preparation for his Thursday job interview.

—

At three o'clock in the afternoon, Uhuru carefully pushed the arched wrought iron gate and walked on the gravel drive to

approach the imposing oak front door of the charming House
of Java, a seventeenth century manor house that still boasted of
many original features. Surveying the magnificent grandeur of
the red brick house, Uhuru supposed that the original owner
must have been a nobleman, someone from the House of Orange perhaps. He would later learn that a one Mr. Runderpan, a
native of Middleburg, who had amassed a fortune in the slave
trade before diversifying into the equally lucrative spice trade,
had commissioned the house in 1799, a time when the fortunes
of the United Dutch East India Company were faltering. The
large neatly kept garden that would be his turf, if he were to get
the gardener appointment, was populated with ancient looking
trees and shrubs. There were several well-placed terraces in the
garden that betrayed romantic tastes. Never before had Uhuru
been in close proximity of such classical opulence, and he had
only known of spacious luxury such as this as something one
read about in leisure magazines depicting the lives of the super rich. It didn't take a degree in Siberian rocks to appreciate
the considerable wealth of the owners of this Kralingen manor
house.

Behind a curtain on the upper floor of her house, Inge Baleman-Ruyter studied the tall, strongly built man walking on the
gravel path. He was the image of masculinity chiseled to its best.
Sprightly steps, long and sure, and yet, she observed, in spite of
his fast pace, there was an element of slowness about his car-
riage. Inge supposed she saw patience in the man, a willingness
to slow down and be taught the ways of the Western world.
She had all along known it would be a black man. That much
had been evident from his foreign accent on the phone. Unlike some people in her circles, she didn't distrust black people,
but again, neither had she dealt with one before. One read all
sorts of disturbing stories about blacks and other ethnic minorities in the papers those days. Much was written about the
increase in crime and drug trafficking that was squarely and
unequivocally attributed to the refugees bundled in a camp on

the fringes of the city. Refugees, immigrants, ethnic minorities, and both petty and hardcore criminals were the same thing to most Dutch, Inge reflected.

She quite didn't comprehend why she had agreed to this afternoon's interview being that she had to reschedule her golf for much later that day. Perhaps it came down to the day prior to the man's call when she had felt disillusioned after missing a short putt for par, and therefore wasn't keen on being on the green. She enjoyed spending time on the nearby nine-hole golf course, swinging her arms and practicing to hit her drives longer and straighter.

In spite of his nonchalant agility, Inge found herself considering the man on her gravel path at once pitiable and savagely sensual. What was his personal story, she wondered? She was eager to know more about this black man and his catalogue of forbidding misery. Was she just being curious out of interest or was she being sadistic? Or did this statuesque stranger smite her? She didn't have much time to reflect on this, as she was summoned downstairs by the loud pinging of the doorbell.

As the front door opened, Uhuru found himself towering over a skinny handsome woman of middle height in a red boob tube top, tight bleached denim jeans, and crimson pointed toe shoes. The generous size of Inge's bust reminded Uhuru of Dolly Parton. He supposed that she was in her fifties. He was quick to observe that she had the gait and ease of a thirty year old. Her long hair that fell in soft gentle curls about her shoulders was blonde. The tanned mature face with fine wrinkles was stern but there was a decisive pleasantness about her brown eyes. The corners of her pink painted full lips were slightly drawn downwards, giving a hint of aristocratic delicateness. She would later confide to Uhuru that her family traced its roots to a nobleman that had ridden side-by-side with Prince William of Orange on numerous battlefields in Flanders, pledging his life and honor to the cause of liberating the Low Countries from Spanish influence.

59

"Ukuulu?" Inge inspected him as if he was an inferior product at the grocers. Uhuru had barely nodded when she continued, "Do I pronounce your name correctly?"

"Uhuru." He articulated slowly, very slowly.

"Sounds rather exotic to me," she said, as if one disapproving of the difficulty of pronouncing foreign names, "Okay, Uhuru, step right in." She threw her head to the left to remove a lock of hair in the face. She led the way and Uhuru followed that fragrance of a sensual scent he had never smelled before, but one which, he perceived, hovered about high society ladies. The entrance was spacious and decorated with potted plants and sculptures. Its massiveness was such that its high walls easily accommodated an oil painting. Not able to draw significant meaning from the brush strokes and flourish of colors, Uhuru supposed the painting was a piece of abstract expressionism. The vastness of the living room and the tidiness of the modern furniture on a massive teak floor bespoke volumes about a lifestyle rich in comfort. The hand of sophisticated taste was evident everywhere. From the high ceiling with the ornamental patterns to the large windows that gave the entire environment an air of romantic asceticism. If he had ever thought of their apartment a shabby hovel, then the splendor of the well-lit spacious interior of House of Java and its expensive furniture forced him to the conclusion that their apartment was a disgraceful pigsty. The living room was the prettiest room he had ever set eyes upon, and he wondered how anybody, short of being a corrupt president of an African country, could maintain a house to such a degree of perfect beauty.

"Have a sit. Coffee?"

"Oh, I am alright. Thank you, madam," Uhuru said politely, as he sat rather uneasily on the edge of a large red sofa, like a long-standing sufferer overwhelmed by the sudden abundance of comfort. Yes, he was thirsty and felt like a cup of tea. But he didn't know if this offer for coffee might be a ploy. He just didn't have the faintest idea on how best to behave before this elegant woman in order to pass the interview.

"Something cold to drink then ... I do insist!" Inge declared with firm finality.

Uhuru did not wish to create an impression of one too demanding. "Apple juice, madam."

"Apple juice!" Inge repeated in the amused tone of one that had come to associate apple juice with children or the sick. "Now that is one thing I don't have in this house. Will orange juice do?"

"Yes, madam," Uhuru answered, rather too eagerly.

Presently Inge returned with a glass of orange juice for both herself and Uhuru. She sunk her light body in a low chair so modern that even Uhuru's undisguised curiosity at the immortality of affluence had problems recognizing it for what it was. Jan des Bouvrie design, he supposed. Thus seated and facing Uhuru, she told him more about the gardener's job before concluding, "It is not a permanent appointment, but there is more than enough work." Inge relaxed back in her chair and crossed her legs. She then chatted a bit about the spring weather, and how welcome it was after the unusually bitter winter. Then she proposed they take a look at the garden.

They walked around the garden with Inge providing a running commentary on this plant and that shrub. And Uhuru made sure (as he had been coached by Amadu) to compliment Inge on keeping such a splendid garden. Amadu had warned him not to overdo the praises. "Reserve that for schizophrenic dictators back home!" After they had toured the large garden, an exercise that took about twenty-five minutes, Inge had formed a pretty good picture of Uhuru.

"And how old are you, Uhuru?" Inge asked with penetrating candor.

"Thirty-four." Uhuru's thoughts momentarily took him to his sweet Mapenzi, who was as old as he was. He couldn't wait to talk to her again and tell her of his new job. Of course, he wouldn't reveal anything about his being a gardener. That was too degrading, he felt. Better to create an impression it was a comfortable job in an office, working with computers and other high tech appliances. That way he could justify the long years of separation from her.

"Well, the job is yours, if you feel up to the challenge." Inge turned her eyes to her long pink glossy fingernails, briefly conjuring up sensual images of intimate moments with a thirty-four year old black man.

"You are offering me the job!" Uhuru could hardly believe his luck.

"Thought you were looking for work, young man!"

"Thank you very much, madam!" Uhuru said exuberantly. "When can I begin, madam?"

"Now." Inge casually ran her fingers through her hair. "There are too many fallen leaves on the gravel path, and if I were you that is where I would begin. By the way do you smoke?"

"Yes, madam." A flicker of disturbing anxiety swept across Uhuru's face.

"There are anti-smoking laws in this country, and I happen to religiously subscribe to them. You shan't be expected to smoke in the workplace. That basically means there will be no smoking on the compound. But that doesn't stop you from smoking once you are out of this fence. I do hope I am clear on that one."

"Yes, madam," Uhuru said, in a subdued voice.

"And for goodness' sake will you stop calling me madam! You make me feel as if I am a senile octogenarian! You can call me Inge."

"Yes, Inge," murmured Uhuru. Up till now he had never addressed any Dutch woman anything other than madam, and jumping this barrier, and more so before a middle-aged woman, came across as rather inappropriate and too familiar. Inge let out a whinny laugh.

"I'll show you the tool shed now."

Inge led Uhuru to a building he had supposed was a guest wing. When they were in the tool shed, Inge said, "All the tools that you shall need are in here ... there is also a kitchenette and bathroom. I never lock up the place so you can always access it.

Just close the door when you are done. I seem to forget something … oh, yes! The first aid box is on the shelf over there." She climbed on a ladder and brought the first aid box down. She opened it to show Uhuru its contents. There were bandages, Elastoplasts, a bottle of disinfectant (iodine, thought Uhuru), forceps, and scissors. "You never know when you might need these," Inge said with tenderness. *How thoughtful and far-sighted*, thought Uhuru! She had thought about possible emergencies and was well-equipped to deal with them. Uhuru had yet to come across an employer who took the welfare of those under her charge seriously. And this made him appreciate Inge's kindness and consideration all the more. It was then that he knew he was going to like this House of Java job more than any that he had hitherto held. He cast his eyes skywards and silently thanked the Lord for this job.

———

That evening a pleased and ecstatic Uhuru invited Amadu, Greg, and Pierre to a treat in an Ethiopian restaurant in downtown Rotterdam where they feasted on *injera* bread with a finely chopped beef sautéed in butter and hot Ethiopian spices. It was in celebration of his new job after a long period of uncertainty. Life would be easy if he were to get some form of permanence, a reliable job that didn't depend on the charity of employers out to exploit a labor force that didn't have a right to argue about low wages. But the prospects of a regular job could only be contemplated if one had legalized his stay in the country, and Uhuru was a realist; he knew that short of a miracle, there would never be a residency permit for him, and hence no regular job. After Uhuru had paid the bill, Pierre suggested they call a cab to drive them to Lounge Cape Verde, a trendy nightclub popular with immigrants.

"No, don't worry," Pierre reassured on seeing the hesitancy on his friends' faces. "I'll pay for the cab."

"What about the entry fee?" Amadu asked. "You would like to pick that one up as well?"

"I am not going near Lounge Cape Verde without Alisi," Greg said firmly.

"Uhuru?" Pierre asked hopefully.

"Not tonight, thanks. Got to work tomorrow."

"It would be a shame if you turned up late at work and that Inge woman fired you on day one of gardening!" Amadu said.

"Oh, tomorrow isn't day one exactly. I already worked this afternoon. Swept the gravel path and watered the potted plants on the veranda. I'll reorganize the tool shed first thing tomorrow. That tool shed is bigger than our apartment, folks! I initially thought it was a guest house. Imagine it has a kitchenette as big as our living room."

"Are you sure about the kitchenette's size?" Greg asked skeptically.

"Okay, not as big as our living room," Uhuru said mortified, "but it is rather big."

"What does her husband do?" asked Amadu.

"I don't know."

"You didn't ask?" inquired Greg.

Uhuru was rather piqued. "Now folks! You surely didn't expect me to put that question to her? Remember she was the interviewer!"

"No need for you to get unnecessarily worked up, dude," Greg said in a reconciliatory tone. "I am equally excited about your job at House of Java. I remember seeing houses in that neighborhood some years ago and thinking, "Boy, those guys are swimming in quid". I only asked out of curiosity, like one African interested in the other."

"Anyone for Lounge Cape Verde tonight?" Pierre asked again.

Nobody was for Lounge Cape Verde. But they agreed it was much better to visit the nightclub on Saturday.

—

Uhuru embarked on his gardening job with a singular determination to succeed. House of Java provided Uhuru a sense of absolute security, which had to do with a deep conviction, misguided as it was, that as long as he busied himself in this splendid garden, there would be no Royal Netherlands Military Constabulary or populist politician dying to deport him. House of Java was a fortified sanctuary, shielded from national bigotry. It was a totally different world among the rhododendrons, apple blossom, magnolias, violets, daffodils, and alliums. Bees hummed hither and thither and birds chirped about in this serene environment of unspoiled grandeur. He developed a fondness for the plants under his care, and through regular visits to the library, came to acquire vast knowledge on gardening. He was surprised that while back at the apartment, he often thought about this or that plant that seemed not to do particularly well. There hadn't been opportunity to talk to Inge since he had got the job. Now and again, he saw her drive in and out of the compound in an off-road gray Volkswagen Touareg. Then there had been a time that she had stopped by, opened the car window, and told him that it was a pity she hadn't got around to chatting with him. She had then said she was off to a luncheon with a friend in Noordwijk aan Zee. Uhuru had thanked her for her generosity, and she had driven off. The next time he saw her was when she was standing behind the large window of what he assumed must have been her bedroom on the second floor. She had waved rather pleasantly, and Uhuru took that as sign of approval for his work. He had yet to see a man in the house and wondered if she was single. Inge Baleman-Ruyter. Her name suggested to him that she was married or even divorced but still keeping her ex-husband's name. Maybe her husband was on a business trip or perhaps worked abroad. That last presupposition he couldn't dismiss because he was exactly in the same position. Perhaps men in Kampala looked at the beauty of Mapenzi and wondered if she was married or divorced! The very thought of that made him laugh aloud. The oddness of laughing alone in the garden made him suspect that anybody seeing him in this state of merriment would surely pronounce him irredeemably insane. Had anybody seen him laugh, he wondered? He turned his gaze to the manor house. Behind the big window, he saw her again. She smiled and waved. He flashed his white teeth and politely waved back. How long had she been standing in that window watching him? A few seconds? One hour? What did it matter anyway? She had every right to supervise him, he reasoned. If she chose to do the supervision from behind a window, then that was perfectly her inalienable prerogative as an employer. Presently she joined him in the garden. She had a pink hooded jacket over a white tee shirt and short red skirt.

"I've brought you your favorite drink." She handed him a glass of apple juice.

"You are so kind, madam."

"Inge. Please call me Inge," she said softly and smiled affably at him. Inge told Uhuru that she liked to see her gardeners feeling at home in the vast compound of House of Java. She then went on to tell him about her last gardener who had been with her for eight years. The man had quit the job because his wife wanted the family to return to their roots in the north. "We called each other by our first names, and that is how I like us to address each other, okay?"

A gardener on first name terms with his employer! *Was she being flirtatious?* thought Uhuru. That was not possible given the wide gulf in their ages he concluded.

"Thank you, Inge," he ventured hesitantly.

"Warm sunny day to be out and about in the garden."

"I do enjoy outdoor pursuits," Uhuru enthused, enjoying the coolness of the apple juice down his throat. "It is entirely suited to my nature." He laughed nervously.

"Shall we sit down?"

They repaired to one of the terraces and sat themselves on cane chairs.

"Do you like living in our country?" She looked him straight in the eye.

Uhuru dropped his eyes. "Yes."

"What is it about the Dutch that you like?"

"Hospitality, friendliness, and their open nature," Uhuru said and dried sweat running down his forehead with the back of his hand. "You can be quite direct, which can't be said of most people."

She laughed. "One rarely hears those qualities being attributed to us ... I mean the affability. I suppose we are as cold as the North Sea wind in winter. Do you have family?" Thoughts of Mapenzi and Juliana flashed through Uhuru's mind, and there was a brief moment of sadness in Uhuru at the long separation from his wife and daughter. These emotions did not escape the focused scrutiny of Inge who took pride in being able to read people's minds.

For a moment, she regretted having put the question to Uhuru. Of course, she thought, he could easily have lost his entire family. Probably, it had been wiped out by machete-wielding men or famine. Perhaps they had perished following a devastating disease epidemic. Hadn't she heard of the deadly Ebola fever in Africa? God knows the tribulations that were visited upon the hapless people of that continent! But Uhuru's hesitation lasted just a moment, and then he answered, "Yes."

There was visible relief on Inge's face as she discovered that her worries were not founded.

"More apple juice or a beer perhaps?" Her smile was warm and encouraging.

"I am alright, Inge." Uhuru was still not entirely confident addressing his employer by her first name. But he was determined to give it a try. All the same Inge walked back to the house and returned with a packet of apple juice.

"Married?" she went on, roundly ignoring his polite protestations as she filled his glass.

"Yes."

"Who is she?"

Uhuru thought she sounded jealous, like she had expected him to reveal he wasn't married. Before he had had a chance to reply Inge quickly added, "She is beautiful, I suppose. African women can be, isn't it? Such full bodies with adorable round hips! But do tell me about her."

For the next few minutes, Uhuru told her about Mapenzi, and Inge couldn't believe that a man could be separated from his wife for such long periods of time. She said she would never accept such an arrangement. And she was particularly devastated when she discovered that Uhuru had a daughter he had never seen.

Inge displayed a sly smile about the corners of her lips. "You must love them a lot. I can see it in your eyes." She couldn't, but under the circumstances, Inge felt she had to say something appropriate as might be expected of an older woman to a young man. Hiding feelings was a high form of civilization, she reflected. But she had to share with him about her troubled past, at least part of it. So she told him that she had once been married and there had been a daughter, Rianne. However, tragedy had struck during the family's annual ski vacation in Lech, Austria. After breakfast Rianne had set off on a snowmobile just like on any other day. Rianne had collided with another snowmobile, sustaining serious head injuries. She had died two days later. "She was eighteen when she died. It was a devastating blow. Marc and I were totally at a loss and didn't know how to cope. But after a long period of mourning, we did manage to rise up and face the world again. Oh, how I miss Rianne and Marc! Yes, I was happily married. Marc was the president of Baleman & Roth, a firm offering investment management to a global clientele. And I ran a florist shop in the fashionable part of Rotterdam … Hillegersberg." She stopped suddenly, let out a long sigh of anguish, stretched her legs, and in the process, her breasts heaved provocatively. There were tears in her eyes. And those tears, a discrete sniff, the white handkerchief delicately mopping at the corner of her eyes hypnotized Uhuru, stirring in him a longing for this woman. She quickly composed herself and presently resumed, "Then Marc was accused of laundering money for South American drug barons. Mind, I did warn him about Frank Hogenhuizen, a scandalously uncaring brute, and begged him not to rubbish off persistent rumors of Frank's possible relationship with the South Americans. Everyone knew then and now that Frank is in soft drugs, and occasionally does ship in kilos of coke. Some years ago with the help of my husband, he acquired House of Piet Snygrens, the fashion store. But people say it was to legitimize his illegal trade. Anyhow, the accusations of money laundering persisted, and police had begun investigating Marc. The pressure was too much, and he thought the best way out was to take his own life." Inge sighed and was on the verge of tears as she recalled the image of her husband with slain wrists. She then spoke of the cremation and the difficult days that followed. But thanks to family and friends, she had been able to overcome the vicissitudes of that period. "It is during that period that I got introduced to art therapy."

Uhuru ventured to ask what art therapy was all about. Inge said it aimed to help people use their inner creativity to help them cope with bereavement or other traumatic experiences. "Through paintings I was able to make my deeper feelings accessible. Anyway, it was a worthwhile exercise, and one that has helped me appreciate works of art." She said that she had now become an avid art collector and also had decided to take up painting and drawing classes, every Monday evening from 8:00 to 10:00 o'clock.

"Life has been so cruel to you."

Inge smiled slowly. "I shouldn't complain, really. Marc left me more than enough money and this beautiful castle. There are those who have had to endure far worse."

Was she taking him into her confidence because she had seen in him the spirit of a warm and caring person? Or was her candor due to emotional anguish at the loss of two beloved and special people? Uhuru grappled with these questions. The widow's tale of vicissitudes had profoundly moved him, and a lump in his throat threatened to choke him. To avert acute suffocation, he swallowed rather hard and loud, which led Inge to turn her sympathetic eyes to him and inquire if all was well. Behind Inge's smiling brown eyes, he could discern embittered melancholy. The tone of her voice betrayed resentful anger at cruel destiny but was empty of self-pity at her solitude. She was a woman determined to go on, to live in the material comfort that surrounded her. Uhuru realized he couldn't remain indifferent to what he had heard. Under normal circumstances, he was an expressive fellow whose life seemed to be ruled by a display of exaggerated gestures, and he suppressed a desire to take her in his arms, to comfort her. But before this woman such a gesture would surely be outright offensive. He hardly understood what he was supposed to do. So he let his silent recognition of her bereavement and his unspoken appreciation of Inge's tragedy fill the quiet that had now settled between them. Inge on the other hand was taken aback by the turn of events.

—

She had started this conversation with the sole and express purpose of gaining more information about the young African's family, and she had geared herself to lend a sympathetic ear to an outpouring of a sorrowful tale. Alas, she had ended up opening her heart, and she was in a state of emotional turmoil, as fresh as that day, four years ago, when Marc committed suicide. She prayed that Uhuru would just offer her a hand, to support her troubled emotions. But Inge knew this was inexpressibly ridiculous. She had just known him a few days, and she couldn't commit her impulses and feelings to the care of a total stranger.

"You have had to endure so much, Inge," Uhuru said with remarkable concern. "I can't do much to ease your pain but I promise to pray for you."

"Oh, prayers!" she shrugged her shoulders as one that does not think much of divine intervention. "I have never gone to church, and I am not a religious person." She went on to emphasize that though not religious, she was a deeply spiritual woman. She dedicated one hour of each morning to classical Yoga. "I do despise that self-righteous Calvinistic austerity that so permeates our society. Life shouldn't be taken too seriously. Unfortunately, there are those holding the view that if one lives on the edge of constant threat of getting submerged under the fiery North Sea, then there is no choice but to take life so seriously to a point of banishing happiness. I am not of that conservative school, my dear."

For days the image of that beautiful mature face with visible traces of vulnerability could not leave Uhuru's mind. He thought of Inge, and in the same breath, thought of Mapenzi. It was as if Inge was the very incarnation of his wife, only grown older, rich, and white. Inge filled his mind and walked in and out of his dreams with relative ease. Was he falling in love with this lonely middle-aged woman? He forcefully dismissed that thought out of his mind.

Chapter 4 Pledge not honored

It was school holiday, and Juliana was running about in the street, playing catch-me-if-you-can with the neighborhood children. There was a lot of screaming and laughing as the children went about their energetic game with unreserved gusto. Not only was Juliana wise beyond her years but she was also tall for her age, which explained her ability to excel at the game, outrunning much older children. Presently she dashed into King Kabaka II Road, with another girl, Gloria, chasing after her.

Lillian, an eight-year old, gestured her to stop. "Juliana!"

"No!" Juliana shouted back. "You want Gloria to catch me, isn't it? Oh, I do know your tricks!"

"No!" Lillian said urgently. "Your mummy is calling you."

"Tricks!" And with that Juliana ran even faster.

"Juliana!" Mapenzi was standing at the junction of King Kabaka II Road and Mahogany Drive. "It is time to go to Auntie Mirembe's office."

This interruption of an enterprise so agreeable didn't wholly amuse the little girl. She stamped her feet down in a show of forceful defiance, "I am not coming!"

"Oh, come on! You don't want to keep your daddy waiting," Mapenzi ignored her daughter's display of temperament. But the mention of the magical word, "daddy," had the effect of wiping away the child's intransigence. She leaped up with joy, and ran towards her mother, shouting, "I am going to talk to Daddy! I am going to my daddy!" And as Juliana sang this cheerful song in celebration of a father she had never seen, other children, with fathers who came home every evening after a long day of laboring in offices and factories, envied one with a father leading an easy life in Europe. In fact, some children with an enviable ability to fantasize were often heard to say that Juliana's father was a white Dutchman, just like Mr. Twiggling (never mind that he was a Briton), the proprietor of Twiddle Dee &

Twiddle Dum Relief Agency for Africa. And some older children who had been toddlers when Juliana's father left for Europe after collecting data for his dissertation claimed that, from what their infantile memories could recall, Uhuru had looked just like Mr. Twiggling, and for all they knew, the two might have been brothers, even twins.

"Hurry!" her mother urged. "We'll be late!"

——

It being the first Tuesday of the month and Juliana on holiday, Mapenzi had conceived the idea of taking Juliana with her to Mirembe's office. Juliana had spoken to her father on numerous occasions in the past, and the very thought of talking to him again filled her with indescribable excitement. Mapenzi combed the child's hair with great care, oiled her face, and dressed her in a pretty striped orange knit dress, the one her father had sent most recently.

And just as they were leaving the house, Juliana remembered she had forgotten to bring her sketchbook. She had been making drawings that she intended to show to Mirembe, whom the little girl liked so much. "My drawings, Mummy!" she said with alarming urgency.

"Where did you leave the book?"

"On my desk." Juliana ran back into the house. Presently, she returned with sketchbook in hand. And as they waited for a minibus to drop them off at the Queen's Tower minibus stop, Juliana wanted to know if her father lived in a huge house with a swimming pool.

"He lives in a high-rise apartment … sixth floor." Mapenzi was proud of this fact.

"Has the apartment got a swimming pool?"

"How often have you asked this question, Juliana?" Mapenzi said with infinite patience. Juliana somehow had it fixed in her little head that her father must have a swimming pool. On several occasions, Mapenzi had told her that one wouldn't have a swimming pool on the balcony of an apartment, but Juliana kept returning to the subject like one who believed that constant broaching of the matter would finally deliver the answer that she wanted to hear. "Why wouldn't people in Europe have swimming pools on their balconies?" Juliana's voice pleaded.

"Because they can't, and that is that, okay?"

"Mummy?"

"Yes?"

"I would like to see my daddy."

"You will talk to him within a few minutes."

"But I want to see him!"

"You can't see him, Juliana."

"Why can't he come to visit us?"

"He can't ... not soon, anyhow."

"Is he in jail like Lillian's papa?" Juliana asked this almost shouting.

"Ssh!" Mapenzi was uncomfortable about her daughter's allusion to Lillian's father. "Your father is in Rotterdam. The Netherlands. Europe!"

"Is Lillian's papa a bad man then?" Juliana asked in all innocence.

"No. He is a political prisoner." Mapenzi looked about them uncomfortably. She was glad there was nobody about to overhear this conversation.

Juliana fixed her steady little eyes on Mapenzi. "What is a political prisoner, Mummy?"

"Now you shut up!" Mapenzi sharply rebuked. She felt she had tolerated her daughter's penetrating inquisitiveness with commendable patience and now was the time to draw the line. The stubbornness of Juliana's persistence often got on her nerves. Her questioning could get persistently irritating, and it was through a supernatural will of effort that Mapenzi resisted the temptation of screaming at her.

———

Mapenzi and her daughter disembarked from the crowded minibus and walked the short distance to Sementi Towers. Bulenda ushered them into Mirembe's office where Mirembe was expecting them. Juliana rushed with her sketchbook to Mirembe who accepted the drawings with a show of exaggerated interest. Mirembe kissed her on the forehead and thanked her for the drawings.

"Which drawing do you like best?" Juliana asked.

"Oh, I do love all the drawings."

"You can't love all things equally," Juliana declared with deep conviction.

"It so happens that I can."

"Nobody can. Not even my father."

Mirembe laughed. "You are too wise for your age, Juliana!"

"Which drawing will it be?"

"Okay, I give up! I like that one." Mirembe pointed to a drawing of a monkey perched on a tree branch.

"Now your turn to tell me and your mummy which is your favorite drawing."

"I like all of them."

—

The two women whiled away the time drinking tea from delicate blue china cups, killing time discussing old acquaintances and talking about Juliana's school. On the other hand, Juliana was contented with being in adult company, at the center of attention. And her beloved Mirembe had made sure there was a cup of cocoa for her.

"So what did you do this morning?" Mirembe asked Juliana, mild curiosity in her voice.

"Oh, played in the street," Juliana said brilliantly and put away her sketchbook. She had been trying to draw Mirembe's office, her desk with its heaps of paperwork being of particular interest.

"Jumped rope?" Mirembe inquired.

"Catch-me-if-you-can," Juliana said proudly and added, "Nobody can catch me because I run much faster than all the other girls."

"I am sure you do, my little darling," said Mirembe with admiration.

Abruptly, Juliana shifted the focus of the conversation to the reason of their presence in Mirembe's office. "Is Papa about to ring?"

"Well, he should be ringing anytime from now, and then you will talk to him," Mirembe said.

"I don't want to go first!" Now that the time of reckoning was about to arrive, the gravity of speaking to a man she had only seen in the family photo album and in the numerous pictures lining their living room wall dawned upon Juliana, making her apprehensive.

The women understood her anxiousness, but were at the same time amused. They laughed and said she needn't worry on that score. Reassured, Juliana bravely announced that she intended to go to spend some weeks with her papa in the Netherlands, during the next school holiday.

"I must warn you," Mirembe said, "it is very cold out there."

"I know. Mummy says it is colder than our freezer."

"Only in winter," Mapenzi said. "Heaps of fluffy white snow everywhere, just like on that beautiful Christmas postcard Daddy sent us last December."

Juliana's curiosity was roused by tales of snow. "Why doesn't it snow here?"

"Because that is the way God has willed it," Mapenzi answered readily. How often she had heard her daughter ask this question!

"Shall I ask Bulenda to bring more tea?" Mirembe inquired. Then she turned to Juliana. "Another cup of cocoa, my dear?"

Mapenzi declined more tea but Juliana nodded her head to the suggestion of more cocoa and even asked, "Can I also have a sweet?"

"Of course, Juliana! Only if your mother consents. Bad for your teeth, you know? Else we'll have to take you to the dentist again!"

"Mummy, just one sweet. Please!" Juliana beseeched her mother, who grunted her consent.

Neither Mapenzi nor Mirembe were completely at ease. For at a quarter to five, there had been no ringing of the phone, which was expected. What jolted them most was the failure of the telephone to ring at five o'clock. There had been a telephone call at ten past five, which had brought cheerfulness and an atmosphere of expectation in Mirembe's office. But it wasn't Uhuru. It was Mr. Frederick Katwe who wanted to know about one or the other dossier. Now it was approaching six o'clock, and most employees had left the building. Mapenzi's gaze was fixed on the telephone. She was horrified by the failure of that piece of technology to utter its characteristic shrill sound that had on all previous occasions brought a thrill to her heart and comfort in her loneliness. Fifteen minutes later there was no word from Uhuru. Mapenzi sighed as the high spirits of a while earlier dissipated to give way to a dark gloom of despondency.

"Odd!" Mapenzi proclaimed. "It has never happened before." It didn't matter to her that she was stating the obvious but for the benefit of keeping to her sanity such words had to be spoken.

"Still early in Rotterdam, my dear," Mirembe said. But she said this with little conviction, like one inwardly convinced Uhuru wouldn't ring that day.

Mapenzi dreaded to think that something serious might have overcome her husband. How she wished he had an email account, then she would surely have asked Mirembe to drop him a line! On several occasions Mirembe had urged them to embrace electronic mail, but Mapenzi and Uhuru had insisted they preferred to talk to each other, to hear the other breathe. Perhaps, thought Mapenzi, this bad experience would encourage them to embrace the convenience of email after all. Then Mapenzi briefly wondered why Watoto Inc. had not thought of turning itself into a cyber café. Colonel Pokoto Street alone boasted of half a dozen Internet cafes. And she didn't doubt that Rotterdam had an even larger offer of cyber cafes.

Mapenzi bit her lower lip. "You don't suppose something is the matter. I mean … not caught up in snow. An avalanche or something like that!"

"Of course not!" There couldn't be snow problems. It is springtime, my dear."

Juliana could feel the sense of unease that permeated the room. "Mummy, isn't Papa going to ring?"

"I asked you to shut up your big mouth!" Mapenzi screamed. This was the first time that Mapenzi had shown such harsh rebuttal to Juliana in Mirembe's presence, and the little girl burst out in tears.

"Sorry, baby," pleaded Mapenzi in a mild tone. "I didn't mean to be rude. Now do come and sit on Mama's lap." But Juliana refused to be bribed into silence by sweet reconciliatory words. Instead she hollered like one being tortured.

"I want my Daddy!" Juliana yelled.

Mapenzi had a burning impulse to reach out to her daughter, to stroke her hair and wipe those tears of infantile frustration. But symptoms of frustration and anger at ruination of a scheme elaborately planned immobilized her in the seat, and she turned her gaze away from Juliana and focused her concentration on the window. Juliana, thus ignored, continued hollering even louder. The helplessness of her daughter calling for intervention from an absent father compounded by the certainty Uhuru wouldn't ring her that day led Mapenzi to break into an uncontrollable sob of betrayal. Why, she asked herself, did Uhuru fail to ring on this particular day when she had made effort to bring their daughter to speak to him? The high pitched sobbing attracted the attention of Mr. Frederick Katwe, who was engaged in delicate discussions with a top client. He popped his white-haired head in the door, quickly appraised the situation at hand, taking particular note of Mapenzi's bitter tears. He closed the door with the same haste that he had opened it, beating a hurried retreat as if he was a general commanding an army on the brink of an inevitable bloody defeat. For all his excellent credentials as a distinguished lawyer good at resolving business conflicts and fixing leaky deals that nobody had ever given a chance, Mr. Frederick Katwe was ill prepared to deal with a crying woman. So he thankfully left this rather messy task in the competent hands of Mirembe, who looked as cool as a cucumber.

"Here," Mirembe said tentatively to Juliana, "have a lollipop. It will do you lots of good." The little adorable girl accepted the lollipop and promptly stopped sobbing. Mirembe then turned her energy to console her friend, rationalizing why Uhuru might not have managed to ring.

"Floods are quite common in the Netherlands. Below sea level, you know. Perhaps the land is flooded and that surely could interfere with communication lines. But it might very well be a local communication network problem and that Uhuru had been trying to get in touch the entire afternoon. Who knows, he might still be trying! There are a host of factors but we shall surely find out next time he calls. Oh, my intuition tells me he will ring tomorrow and explain this mix up. Don't despair! It is not like he has divorced you! Why don't we pop in at China Wall for an early dinner?" Convinced that tears weren't going to reverse smashed hopes and send telephones ringing, Mapenzi presently composed herself and twenty minutes later they drove to China Wall, ending up at a table that had been reserved for three.

———

At the time that Mapenzi and Juliana patiently waited in Mirembe's office for Uhuru's telephone call, Uhuru was sitting next to Inge in the Volkswagen Touareg returning from an enjoyable trip that had seen them visit a garden center and also share a bench in a public park. That he didn't ring Mapenzi on that first Tuesday of April had everything to do with the turn of events at House of Java. In fact, he had slipped the international telephone calling card into his pocket (their apartment didn't have a telephone) and had contemplated that he would briefly suspend his activities in the garden for not more than twenty minutes, be at a public telephone booth by four o'clock (five o'clock, Mapenzi's time), and chat with his wife, as had been the unbroken tradition. During the lunch break, he had walked about in the neighborhood, and to his horror he couldn't find a public telephone in the vicinity of House of Java! Well, he had thought, he would have to rush to some other place with a telephone booth after work. There was just a chance that even at such a late hour, Mapenzi and Mirembe would still be waiting for his call. That was not to be because in the early afternoon Inge came to him in the garden, where he was engaged in the delicate task of trimming a shrub, and said she wanted him to accompany her to the Intratuin garden center that afternoon. Inge said that he could help her in choosing the plants because she had come to believe he knew so much about gardening.

"I have been observing you tendering the flowers, the violets, and alliums. Oh, the way you hold that watering can! No gardener has ever pruned that tamarisk with such an absorbing sense of care. So much passion and sensitivity… you are a born gardener, Uhuru. How I wish I had found you much earlier!" Inge laughed with a gaiety of spirit that Uhuru had not yet observed in her. She looked longingly at him and then flung her hair back with a delicate swing of the head. The softness of her small white neck suffused him with a thrill of adventure, a desire to feel her skin. The unexpected vote of confidence in his work had been delivered so affectionately and sincerely, Uhuru perceived. He felt that uttering a word short of consenting to Inge's shopping enterprise would be misguided, a dislocation of the bond of warmness and fondness that was fast developing between them. So it was that he responded excitedly, saying he would consider it an honor to accompany Inge to the garden center.

"You are all muscle, so you can help with the bags!" Inge said cheerfully, as she flung her arms in the air.

"I would be delighted to, madam," Uhuru ejaculated wringing his hands with childlike excitement.

"Inge is the name. Must it take centuries for Africans to learn!" she said not unkindly.

It was then that Uhuru realized his folly and laughed. She then retrieved dark glasses from her handbag, and swinging the car keys shouted excitedly to Uhuru, "Let us go to Intratuin, my Masai warrior!" It wasn't in her nature to be a scheming enchanter but she saw no good reason to stop her from pursuing this young man and have him for herself, keep him close to her heart. Possibly with time, she imagined, she could have him move in with her.

However, it wasn't to Intratuin but to another garden center at the outskirts of Gouda that they finally drove to. There weren't many people around and Inge, with the confidence of one that had been here on countless occasions, disclosed that Saturdays were the worst in terms of crowding. "You would be forgiven to think that all the fifteen million Dutch people had been deported into this tiny place. I prefer coming here on weekdays."

"Excuse me." Uhuru maneuvered the trolley away from an elderly couple taking up as much room as possible of the narrow gangway. Inge followed behind, and Uhuru wondered what the people here might make out of him. Perhaps a few might see him for what he was, a young gardener in the pay of a much older rich lady. Others might think that he was Inge's young lover. He recalled that when Milagros Gonzalez still dated the young Dutchman, she had said it was trendy for older women to go for younger men. Amadu had responded by saying that, although he had no principle objections to the ultimate celebration of female liberation, he could hardly see himself shagging anything older than twenty-five. And that came from a forty-nine year old man who had told them of his first sex encounter at a tender age of nine. Amadu came from a wealthy family that could afford employing the services of a maid and giving generous pocket money to the children on their birthdays. Whereas other kids his age used the money got at birthdays and other festive occasions to buy sweets and such toys that captured the fancy of little children, Amadu had kept his francs until they had accumulated to a handsome amount. It was with this money that he had confronted their maid, a fifteen-year-old country girl. She had readily agreed to take the money in return for unbridled sex in the maize barn. The relationship had gone on for months. Then one hot afternoon as Amadu huffed and puffed atop the maid who could not hush her sweet moans, his mother sprang a surprise. Of course the maid was sacked there and then, and the precociously amorous Amadu banished to the hardship of an all-boys boarding school where the only female on the compound was a despotic arithmetic teacher who looked more male than female.

"Oh, don't they have such glorious beauties!" Inge said, as they stood before pots of pink, purple, and white hyacinths.

Uhuru pointed to a row of colorful primroses. "Goes together with those over there."

"No surer sign of spring in the garden than hyacinths and primroses!" Inge consented. She quickly picked up quite some flowers and gently placed them in the trolley. Then she also wanted calla lilies, peonies, begonias, and when they were almost done insisted on offering Uhuru red emperor tulips.

"I don't have a garden … only a tiny balcony," Uhuru said apologetically, disliking every bit of living in an unglamorous block of apartments.

"Well, you can have a portion of my garden for yourself. We'll buy the tulips, as well." With that Inge made it abundantly clear there would be no further discussion about the issue. She added tulips to the near-overflowing trolley.

On their way back, Inge said it would be an honor to show Uhuru something of the Dutch landscape. "I grew up in the country … Poederdorp, that is. In spite of the many years that I have lived in Rotterdam, I still consider myself a country girl. I savor the sheer beauty of cows in the open fields, the serenity of willow trees, and the freshness of unpolluted air. That is why I love the countryside … I always go back to visit my folks in Poederdorp," she said wistfully. "Heard of the place?"

"Why!" Uhuru said excitedly. "The Royal Family will be visiting on Queen's Day, isn't it?"

"Yes, but I do not care much for the Royal Family," Inge said with apparent disinterest in the annual national celebrations at the end of April. "Queen's Day is an opportunity for me to leave the country, a few days holiday in a sunny place. This time we are off to Rome … with Annemarie. But I am impressed you have heard of Poederdorp. Most people I know confuse it with Poederoijen."

"Poederoijen is close to Slot Loevenstein where Hugo de Groot was banished to eternal imprisonment." Uhuru reveled in his knowledge of Dutch history. He thrilled in the thought that he had at last found a Dutch person, an audience, that he could impress on his mastery of his adopted country's history. He might have been an illegal alien before the law but deep inside him he truly saw no reason why he shouldn't belong to and claim part of that long and rich history.

"Oh, I wouldn't know," Inge said with finality and inadvertently disappointed Uhuru. Uhuru thought it was wise to shut up and not pursue Dutch history or geography any further. He was also saddened that Inge didn't show much enthusiasm for the monarchy that he simply adored. Imagine spending Queen's Day in Rome when the Queen was visiting her hometown! Such a lack of patriotism as displayed by Inge greatly disturbed him. Having even bought a flag for the occasion, he was looking forward to Queen's Day and to flying it in full glory from their balcony. The monarchy was so dear to him, an institution of national identity and a source of undying pride. So passionate was he about royalty that besides a passport size photograph of his wife and daughter, he also had photos of his favorite members of the Dutch royal household proudly displayed in his wallet. Now it would be the Queen and on another occasion, depending on his mood, it might be one of the princesses. He had welcomed the latest addition to the ranks of royalty with ecstatic happiness, and the baby, Her Royal Highness, the Princess of the Netherlands, Princess of Orange-Nassau, was a source of inner joy, just like his own Juliana. It was the small snapshot of the baby's pink face, dressed in white, which he happened to carry in his wallet, at that moment. He had found this wonderful photo in the *Rotterdam Weekly Herald* and had promptly cut it out. When Greg and Pierre said he was behaving oddly carrying photos of total strangers, their royalty notwithstanding, he had, in a show of patriotic pride, retorted by citing the centuries old words of Don John of Austria, "The Prince of Orange has bewitched the minds of all men. They love him, and fear him, and wish to have him as their lord."

———

Inge and Uhuru were now driving over a lifting bridge. Presently they were traveling through expanses of flat green scenery littered every so often with sheep and cows. Inge reflected on her childhood in the countryside. "When I was a little girl we would go camping amidst the cows, wakening in the morning to their moos."

Now and again, Inge would stop to exclaim at the sheer beauty of lambs in the field. And in his turn, Uhuru pointed out a rabbit that had darted across the road, disappearing into the tilled field. Then Inge made a stop on a deserted dyke. She had just sighted a beautiful bird, a blue throat, which brought such delight and brightness on her face.

"The birds of spring!" declared Inge wistfully. Inge's head swirled with the lyrics of Cor Lemaire and Annie Schmidt's *The Birds of Holland* where French, Japanese, and Chinese birds sang a monotonous and uninspiring tudeludelu. Nowhere did the birds sing so happily and merrily as in the glorious beauty of a mellow Dutch spring … the nightingale, the thrush, and the blackbird. She wanted to sing this song to Uhuru but the tune eluded her, and besides she was no good at singing. A few minutes later, they took a right turn, drove off the dyke and two or three kilometers down the road, they approached a roadside park. Inge suggested that they should get out of the car in order to be closer to Mother Nature.

"Let's have some fresh air, Uhuru." Inge's eyes burned with the excitement of adventure.

"Good idea!" Uhuru enthused.

Then they got out of the car and stood in silence for a few seconds, as if the solitude of the park might disappear in face of words. The sun was behind them, casting comically long shadows in front of their feet. Inge was weighing in her mind if she should hold Uhuru's hand, but before she was decided, Uhuru put his hands in his trouser pocket, way out of her reach. Not fully happy with standing in silence, Inge eyed a bench. "Oh, let us sit down and have a chat. I really must get to know you better!"

They sat side by side on a wooden bench which still showed visible signs of moss that had found refuge in a winter since gone. And just then they noticed the fading words scrawled on the bench. *Niggers = Cancer.* Those words cut through Uhuru's soul, reminding him that he wasn't entirely welcomed in this country. He was now conscious of a breeze lapping about his body, and he shivered as though hit by the icy northeastern winter wind that swept southwards from its origins in Siberia. Inge was quick to realize his discomfort and expertly steered their attention away from the offensive inscription. And they both succeeded in pretending that they hadn't seen any offending words, picked up the thread of their merry discourse as if racial prejudice could never touch them. They talked idly about the unusually good weather and rejoiced in the beauty of a glorious and serene sunny afternoon. The sweetness of the gentle breeze was rich with delicate scents of a polder landscape bursting forth in celebration of early spring. In front of them was an expanse of green tender grass interspersed with bright yellow coleseed flowers and buttercups, a signature of new life.

"Oh, I do like your shirt," Inge said suddenly, her heart beating about with the thrill of a woman on the edge of falling in love.

"A Mandela shirt," Uhuru said proudly. He wanted to return the compliment, telling her that the short dress she wore was sexy. But he reasoned it would hardly be the right thing to do.

"Mandela?" she repeated with intense interest.

"Nelson Mandela." Uhuru was not sure if Inge didn't know who Mandela was. This wouldn't have come as a surprise to him since she seemed ignorant of Hugo de Groot.

Inge sensed what was going through Uhuru's head. "Of course! I didn't know he had a shirt named after him. I know about roads, however."

A bicycling elderly couple entered the park and momentarily oblivious to the presence of Uhuru and Inge headed for a nearby bench. Upon seeing Uhuru and Inge seated close to each other and their proximity to the empty bench they were set to occupy, the elderly couple mumbled a few apologetic words and were on their way out of there. Uhuru supposed that the couple must have perceived that he was Inge's lover and possibly didn't want to interrupt the serenity of a spring romance.

"Uhuru, do you ever speak to them," Inge asked after the couple had made their exit.

"Sorry?"

Inge turned to face him with a charming smile, and clarified. "The flowers, I mean."

"No," he said slowly, afraid that she might chastise him for a lack of interest in keeping the flowers company.

"Oh, you had better make it a habit," she said cheerfully. "They will respond to that strong booming voice of yours. You should laugh, too. I do quite like your laughter and those wonderful white teeth," Inge said and dusted Uhuru's Mandela shirt as if it had accumulated dirt. She wanted to take full advantage of her proximity to him, deciding to give herself to Uhuru in a most unambiguous manner. And yet this young man could not comprehend her yearning and seize his chance! Seeing that he was rather uncomfortable at her brazen attempt at intimacy, she abruptly changed course and asked, "Tell me about your apartment."

"The apartment belongs to Greg Okafor, an African immigrant. I sub-rent a bedroom."

"How terrible! It is like living in a student's apartment, isn't it? Sharing a common bathroom and kitchen ... Oh, my! I wouldn't think of it."

"There is also Pierre Kalongo," Uhuru said in an animated tone.

Inge was alarmed. "Three adults sharing one apartment?"

"Yes," Uhuru said in a timid voice. He had been unaware that Inge couldn't comprehend three adults squeezing in one apartment and now felt a sense of unease at volunteering this information.

"You should get your own place." Inge's tone of voice suggested if he had his own place she would not care about visiting him and perhaps trying out a naughty thing or two.

"It is fun, really. The boys are such a terrific team. We have never quarreled amongst ourselves ... I mean nothing big, and we do have a close-knit relationship built on mutual respect. I do rather enjoy it."

"Okay. But it also has its downside, doesn't it? It means you can't have a private moment with your own visitors!" Inge was used to being dotted with the privileges and material comfort that money could buy.

"Not quite. When Greg and Alisi ...," Uhuru began. On realization that Inge wouldn't know Alisi, he quickly added, "Alisi is Greg's girlfriend, you see. When they want privacy they retreat to their bedroom, and we folks, Pierre and I, know that that is their sacred sanctuary. We don't bother them at all."

"Rightly so. Unless of course if you are into orgies and that sort of thing."

"Oh, no!" Uhuru said hurriedly. Now, if he had been light of color he would have blushed with profound embarrassment. Thanks to his melanin full skin, he managed to conceal his discomfiture in the face of Inge's relentless candidness.

"So you entertain your female visitors in your bedroom, eh?" Inge studied his face intensely. She didn't mind that he had a wife in Africa, a historical accident that she couldn't reverse.

Inge felt she could not stand it if Uhuru were to tell her of a girlfriend he regularly entertained in his Rotterdam bedroom.

"I do not get visitors as a matter of fact," Uhuru said truthfully and ignored her allusion to women.

"How come, Uhuru?" Inge's relief suffused through her entire body. She wanted to unearth everything about this man that she found so endearing.

"I haven't been in this country long enough."

"No friends, shall I presume?" Inge observed his reaction with a serene intensity which was at once absorbing and indulging.

"In a sense Greg's and Pierre's friends are my friends, too ... even Alisi's friends. That is the nature of Africans and their social circles."

Inge was genuinely amused. "Funny! My husband's friends were his and not mine. And the contrary was true. I have shared so much with Annemarie, and yet my husband only got to know her on a very superficial level. I often suspected that Marc didn't exactly like my female friends. But neither did I care for that Frank Hogenhuizen, a man he held in high esteem."

Uhuru found himself telling her about the party at the apartment with Greg's ex-Yugoslav friends and how he had managed to get Inge's address. "So it is through Greg's social network that I ended up getting this precious gardener job."

Inge laughed, a relaxed laugh. "Truly amazing tale, Uhuru. I am glad that Goran fellow led you to the warmth of House of Java! Welcome, Uhuru!" She then stretched her legs and threw them carelessly wide apart. A frantic desire to be kissed by those large black lips burned through her and her generous breasts rose and fell in waves of longing. Uhuru couldn't resist stealing a look at those lovely breasts. His gaze floated on Inge's chest for longer than he had intended, settling on the profile of the taut nipple like barren Sahara dust violently pushed northwards before coming down gently on the fertile Dutch polders. A smile of satisfaction crossed Inge's face as she caught Uhuru's eyes hovering hungrily over the ampleness of her breasts. She was glad for the low cut neckline of her dress and the breast enlargement operation in an exclusive private Swiss clinic, a short drive out of Montreux. *Yes!* she silently craved, *Seize your chance, African boy! You can touch my breasts and fondle my nipples if you want.*

However, the African seemed petrified into docility, frightened to embrace the warmth of sensual femininity. On sensing Inge had seen his fugitive eyes resting voraciously on that all conquering manifestation of female sexuality, Uhuru quickly glanced sideways to hide embarrassment that was rising up like bile in his chest. Were those penetrating eyes seducing him? Having the disadvantage of inexperience at his side in delicate matters of this nature, he didn't want to believe that Inge was going out of her way to tempt him! How he longed for a cigarette to bring clarity to a clouded mind! The last thing he ever wanted to do was to misinterpret the generosity and warmth of one that had taken him off the street. And yet there was that unmistakable carnal look in Inge's eyes! She had somehow moved closer to him, and he didn't find this closeness totally disagreeable. On the contrary, there surged into his body a strong urgency, a brute need so long suppressed, to take a beautiful woman into his arms. If at that moment Uhuru had been conscious of the commonality of their minds, he would have kissed Inge passionately, his hands stroking her loose blonde hair. And without quite understanding the impulse, Uhuru's eyes overcame their shyness and he looked at Inge. Their eyes locked briefly in a conspiracy of shared amorousness, and he saw Inge's face glow with the elation of a venturous spirit awaiting the final call to embark on a journey of sensual exploration, a ride on the waves of lustfulness. But just then there was an interruption, rudely stopping the actors in this play of evolving passion. A family of four came cycling noisily into the roadside park, obviously too keen to sit down and unwrap their sandwiches. And the father chose to sit his wife and children, kids of five and nine, on the very bench that the elderly couple had avoided out of respect for the lovers. A low flying KLM jet tore through the sky, adding

to the racket of the four new arrivals and completely shatter-
ing Uhuru's focus on the grail of corporeal desire. Now Uhuru's
eyes blinked and disengaged from Inge. A shade of hesitation
crossed his mind, and the courage that he had somehow summoned from a place he didn't quite comprehend deserted him,
leaving him deflated like a punctured inflatable sex doll. What
could they do? Uhuru and Inge could not order the intruders
out of the public park. They recomposed themselves and remained seated on the bench for a little while as if waiting for the
sunshine to die from the distant horizon.

"I could sit here forever," Inge said and reflected on the pleasurable sensation that had momentarily inflamed her body and
burned into her soul.

"Me, too," Uhuru enthused, as he enjoyed the beauty of the
flat landscape and the scent of spring.

"We should be returning to Rotterdam, Uhuru, or else I will
be late for Annemarie's birthday! I'll take you to Kinderdijk,
someday. Then you will see the wonders of Dutch technology!"

"Windmills, right?" Uhuru stood up.

"Been there?" Inge inquired, as they walked to the car.

"No," Uhuru said and shook his head. "But I have read about
Kinderdijk." Yes, in his quest to become a Dutchman, Uhuru
had practically read everything about the Netherlands. They
headed back to Rotterdam, behind them the polder settling
down to its rhythm of solitude.

—

"Ladies and gentlemen we will shortly be landing at Schiphol
Airport. Kindly fasten your seat belts and make sure your seat
and tray table are in an upright and locked position ..." The
mellifluous voice of Milagros Gonzalez floated in the Business
Class cabin of the 747 jet from Bangkok, which was scheduled
to touch down at Schiphol fifteen minutes earlier than planned.
But one passenger with roguish blue eyes half-closed and mind
reveling in his latest trip to Thailand didn't bother to do any
of these things that Milagros was requesting of the esteemed
Business Class passengers. The rather heavy man wore a dark

blue business suit, and the grayness of his short cropped hair was distributed around the temples and nape of his neck. He was keen about keeping healthy and jogged five kilometers on most mornings, and when not traveling, visited the gym thrice a week. This rigorous attention to a routine of regular exercise helped him maintain an excellent form. That explained why most people underestimated his age, thinking he was in his mid-forties. In fact, he was fifty-nine.

Frank Hogenhuizen was returning from an eight day business trip to Bangkok but as usual had made sure that there was lots of pleasure. The first thing that he had done on arriving in Bangkok was to ring an old acquaintance, Adrian Slangenveld, an independent business consultant advising a number of European and American companies in South East Asia. Adrian had lived in Thailand for over a decade, and as always had seen to it that a boy was available for Frank's pleasure. The lad must have been fifteen or sixteen. He didn't really care about the boy's age. The younger they were the better. The encounter had been memorable albeit a little exhausting. But after a long day of hard negotiations with tiring business associates, Frank had looked forward to exploring the lad's body. And the boy had faithfully showed up at his hotel each evening.

The first night he had been so hungry for the boy that he had not given him time to undress. He had rushed towards the receptive body, violently tore the boy's tight trouser and had proceeded to satiate himself with overwhelming brute force. It had given him a sense of enormous pleasure and a feeling of power as he heard the little slim lad's whimpering plea to slow the pace of his burning enthusiasm. Instead of leading him to gentleness, the boy's muffled groans of pain had driven Frank to more aggression, his hugeness thrusting deep and punishing the boy with renewed brutality. He thought of the boy's frightened face on the last evening, and a malicious delight permeated his body. But that was Bangkok, and here he was about to land at Schiphol.

After such an agreeable experience in Bangkok, he couldn't say he was looking forward to seeing Nicole, his wife of twenty-three years of marriage. However, he reflected that he had missed chocolate sprinkles at breakfast (one quickly gets tired of the uninspiring continental buffet breakfast staple of five-star hotels) and also his nineteen-year-old daughter, Sylvie. She was a first year law student at Leiden, and Frank simply adored her. He pulled at the knot of his Thai silk tie, and then his mind lingered back to the Thai boy. A disturbing thought crossed his mind. Suppose Sylvie was to fall in love with a fifty-year old man or be forced to sleep with a man as old as her father for the sake of earning a little pocket money? Not that he doubted his daughter, a decent and intelligent girl with high class upbringing, but the very thought of the ideas playing about in his mind stirred him to such terrific panic. If it hadn't been for the fact the plane was landing shortly, he would have ordered that black stewardess with the long legs to pour him a large brandy. He needed it to steady his terrified nerves. Instead he made do with swallowing hard, running a trembling hand through his thinning hair, and looking out of the window to confront the meticulously partitioned flat landscape of various shades of geometrical shapes. He regretted not having prolonged his stay in Bangkok, something he could have done with relative ease. However, he had to return home to talk to his bank. He desperately needed three million euro to purchase a luxurious tourist resort in Thailand to further legitimize his business concerns, and at the same time, more significantly, an important source of funds to support his other ailing investments. But he was a little apprehensive if the bank would honor his request this time round, since he owed it enormous sums. All the same, he was glad that he had a faithful and discrete man such as Adrian Slangenveld on his side. It was Adrian who had alerted him to this exciting investment. Milagros walked down the aisle, and with a false broad smile delivered in a manner that can only be perfected by Business Class stewardesses, politely but firmly asked Frank to fasten his seat belt.

Back on the polder landscape, Uhuru looked at that plane as it prepared its landing at Schiphol. The jet gave no hint that perhaps one of the passengers in its bowels would influence and even direct the affairs of Uhuru's life. It just flew on, as Uhuru watched it trace a well-charted path of descent, disappearing from the radar of his vision. Uhuru was seized by a strong desire to run away from the ensnaring presence of Inge and fly to Mapenzi and Juliana. He had come close to betraying them, but thanks to the intervention of the rowdy family of bicyclists and the droning noise of the KLM jet, had not.

Chapter 5 Friends deliver a verdict

"A sliver of apple cake, my dear," Inge said to Annemarie with delightful modesty. Annemarie van Eldijk was a woman on the plump side and blessed with an extraordinarily pretty and youthful round face. Her hair, which was short, wavy, and dyed pink, was the only surviving physical testimony of teenage years spent in the embrace of the Amsterdam squatter movement. On this particular evening, she wore white stretch pants and a poncho with red, brown, and pink stripes. She had offered Inge a choice out of three different delicious tarts, specially ordered for her birthday. She had turned fifty-five, was rich, and recently divorced from a Hilversum film producer she had lived with for fifteen years. She had won the battle of staying in their 1903 grand villa in Noordwijk aan Zee, a stone's throw away from the enchanting North Sea seaside.

"Good choice, Inge!" Annemarie enthused. "The cherry is equally good, dear." One of the guests in the crowded room said he was eating apple cake, and he would surely recommend it. "A piece of art, Annemarie," he added for emphasis. Other apple cake eaters nodded their heads in agreement.

As Inge ate her cake and sipped coffee, she made conversation with old acquaintances but she found the entire evening stale in spite of the delightful voices all around her. She indeed tried to throw all her attention to these cheery voices but she found herself lacking the conviction to laugh as heartily as the others when a joke was made or someone narrated a particularly silly episode. Seeing Annemarie enter the kitchen, Inge saw her chance to talk to her away from the others. Inge joined Annemarie in the kitchen. Indeed Annemarie hadn't had time enough to chat with all her friends, but that was part of birthday celebrations. The celebrant was continuously on her feet, making sure there were enough eats and drinks going round and that each of the invited guests was comfortable.

"You look exhausted, Inge! Are you all right?" Annemarie asked.

"You shouldn't worry about me, dear. I haven't felt any better!"

"Glad to hear that, my dear. And how did you fare with Henk?"

Inge laughed. "No better than last time."

Henk Koopmans was a tall overweight man with a long face and a complexion nearly devoid of color. He reminded Inge of someone tormented by years of indigestion. Henk was a real estate agent, widowed and about Inge's age. Annemarie, in her self-appointed role as matchmaker, had been making brave attempts to couple Inge with Henk ever since Marc died. Although he was kind and considerate, Inge found him totally uninspiring, not her dish, really. Henk was at once taciturn and demanding. If you didn't say anything to him, he said nothing to you. And if you played his taciturn game, he looked at you with big accusing eyes, as if you were hiding something from him that he had a right to know of. It was hard to see how the man had become a successful real estate agent. Inge had come to a conclusion that he was best served by a wife who was willing to lead a more conventional, traditional lifestyle. What Henk needed, Inge had told Annemarie after a difficult one and half hours visit to his Blaricum mansion some weeks earlier, was a wife contented to wait in the shadow of her husband's successful business empire, welcoming him from a hard day's work with a wholesome dinner of pork chops, beans, and boiled potatoes. And to make matters worse, fishing was his idea of a hobby, and Inge loathed men that fished, since she imagined the marine object of their fascination was the only thing that counted in their lives.

"He is respectable," Annemarie said. "Henk is a true Dutch gentleman of the old school."

"No question about that," Inge said sympathetically. "He isn't just my type."

"What is your type of man?"

"It is certainly not Henk Koopmans! But there are some important matters I would like to talk to you about later."

Inge consulted Annemarie on both grave and insignificant matters. Annemarie was full of advice, and although Inge found much of it totally worthless, she nevertheless, out of years of habit, always turned to her. And in this enterprise with Uhuru, she sought Annemarie's approval, in spite of knowing that even if Annemarie disapproved, she would still go ahead and seduce Uhuru.

"We can chat now if you so wish." Annemarie nodded, indicating they could discuss the matter right there in the kitchen.

"No. We will need a private moment, away from all this."

"Okay. Let's go upstairs then. I really don't mind, and you know that!"

"That would be dreadfully unfair to your visitors. We need some time together, just the two of us and out of ear shot."

"Anything serious I should be worrying about?"

Inge smiled. "Not at all, my dear."

"Let's see …" Annemarie ran her mind over her busy schedule. "I've got to be at the hairdresser on Monday morning. Then take Erozan to the vet …"

"Erozan?" Inge said with alarm. Erozan was a Bedlington terrier that had been with Annemarie for a number of years, and she was fiercely attached to the dog.

"She has eye problems and poor appetite. She has lost weight and does not like to go out for her evening walk. I am quite worried about her."

"Where is she?"

"I took her to my nephew for the day. I didn't want her getting upset by all the people and activities here."

"It is not something that a vet can't fix, I am sure," Inge said with confidence.

"Tests have been done, and the results should be in sometime soon." Annemarie fervently hoped that whatever was bothering Erozan, it wasn't anything serious like cancer. In fact her mind had been so focused on the possibility that her dog might have cancer or an equally dreadful terminal illness. She couldn't imagine living in a world without Erozan; it was too painful to contemplate. And since the break up of her marriage, she had begun to appreciate even more the loyalty of her dog. A man would very easily behave stupidly, causing extreme emotional distress to his wife; but a dog remained true to her owner. Yes, it had been Paul, and not Erozan, that had acted insensitively forcing Annemarie to make the decision that saw him leave the house.

"Poor Erozan!" Inge said, deeply touched by the dog's ailment. Annemarie's eyes moistened at this show of empathy from her friend, and she blew her nose noisily into a paper tissue.

"I think she … she will …" Annemarie's voice choked with emotion, and Inge moved closer to her and placing a comforting arm on her shoulder. Annemarie appreciated that display of support and presently pulled herself together and finished off her sentence, "She will be all right, Inge. Oh, you are such a sweet dear! Why don't you come over next week … Friday afternoon? Then we can have a stroll on the seaside if the weather permits. I fear we might miss Erozan's company. You aren't playing golf on Friday, by any chance?"

"The golf course is undergoing renovation …," Inge said, "… drainage improvement. It was rather soggy the last time I was on the green."

"Is Friday okay with you then, about three o'clock?" Annemarie didn't really care about golf and failed to understand why Inge had not taken up horse riding or polo. She was an ardent horse rider and played polo with gusto.

"Got a Friday morning appointment with my manicurist after which I will lunch with Katrine. Three o'clock should work out just fine."

—

On Friday morning before leaving the house to get her nails done, Inge stood at the wide tall window of her bedroom, surreptitiously behind a curtain, observing the subject of her interest pushing a wheelbarrow filled with cypress mulch. It was the first time that she had seen him bare-chested, and that sight brought a yearning so profound, assailed her body with a lustful ravenousness and her innards burned with uncontrollable sexual desire. She found herself going through an involuntary motion of removing her lace-trim thong, and she was glad the era of chastity belts was long since gone. She badly wanted to lay naked beside him, making love for much of the day and through the entire night. She now visualized herself in a black lace G-string and garter belt and spike-heeled black boots, bending before him and ready to welcome Uhuru's massive blackness. Then she instinctively started stroking the inside of her thigh, gradually moving her fingers to the softness between her legs, rhythmically rubbing her warm wetness. Then she lifted the wet finger to her nostrils, smelling the scent of wild passion. There was a fire in her eyes, a recklessness she had not known in years. She felt no sense of embarrassment as her body stiffened and then loosened. She wriggled and panted in the joyful throes of wild ecstatic passion, and her body shook in spasmodic waves of pleasure. The sheer weight of exhaustion forced her to collapse on the carpeted floor. Uhuru, she conceded, had aroused her body out of sensual retirement, and she was pleased to have masturbated because of him. Yes, she needed Uhuru desperately, and if it meant putting a ring through her nipples or some other delicate place on her body to win his love, she would have happily obliged.

Inge recalled with eternal fondness the shared moment of the previous week on the park bench with Uhuru. His laughter had suffused warmness in her body, and she swore there was a certain erotic twang about it. For three consecutive nights she had dreamt about that lovely afternoon, waking up each time as she came to within inches of an orgasm, a delightful experience she had not known in a very long time.

After watching Uhuru go about his garden duties for twenty or so minutes, Inge felt an enormous emotional exhaustion weighing so heavily on the body that the only logical outcome was a physical strain, which fatigued every single muscle fiber. She stood up from her secret hiding position, stretched her arms and legs, surrendering to the reality of his presence in her life. She was glad that she was seeing Annemarie that afternoon, and who knew? Perhaps she might share a tip or two on how best to seduce an African man! After all, she was a woman that loved surrounding herself with men, and it was common knowledge that she had slept with quite a few of Paul's friends. There had even been a rumor of her doing a disappearing act while she and Paul vacationed in the Gambia. It was said she had slept with a black man. But Paul wasn't a saint either, as far as Inge could tell. His credentials as a man that had difficulties keeping his pants on were legendary. And yet that wanton display of unfaithfulness wasn't the reason for their divorce. The singular reason for the couple's divorce was a hamster.

Paul had never been keen on animals, although he grudgingly walked Erozan now and again. Annemarie swore that Erozan was very much aware of his disinterest in her, encouraging Paul to adopt a more animal friendly attitude. Perhaps it was this constant nagging that had led him to decide to own a pet. He had settled for a hamster. As it was the hamster was pregnant, giving birth ten days later to nine babies. When Annemarie had inquired what he intended to do with the litter, he had replied rather cheekily that he would flush them down the toilet. Then seeing the hurt in Annemarie's eyes he had laughed, dismissing the whole idea as a big joke. Indeed when the hamsters were a few weeks old, he had gone through the trouble of buying cages for them, which greatly pleased Annemarie. But then he had also discovered another favorite pastime sport, which he kept concealed from his wife. He bought rat traps and with intense relish released the hamsters one by one, cheering at the hamsters' demise. Mutual infidelity Annemarie could stand but callousness and unparalleled brutality to harmless rodents was too much to stomach. She bundled Erozan in the car, headed to a solicitor, and swiftly filed for divorce, citing marital infidelity on the part of Paul.

As Inge drove out of House of Java to meet Katrine and finally visit Annemarie, she waved enthusiastically to Uhuru, whom she had not yet had an opportunity to speak to during the entire week. On Monday, just as she was scheming to invite him inside for tea, there were developments that forced her to keep mostly indoors, spending much of the time in bed perusing through her old copies of *Viva, Seasons,* and *Quote,* and in between, reading and watching television. (She had to admit there wasn't anything interesting on television those days; not even reality television's latest program, Imbeciles, featuring a group of people floating on a plastic mat in the middle of a kidney-shaped swimming pool. The winner was the one that gave the most idiotic answer to questions put by a panel of slalom canoeing enthusiasts around the world.) She was even forced to cancel her Monday evening art lesson, explaining to the art teacher that she was indisposed. Her words were carefully crafted to suggest a touch of flu. The art teacher was very kind about it, considering that she had been absent from class for two consecutive Mondays and had taken it upon himself to suggest rest before wishing her quick recovery. This self-imposed period of rest and postponement of regular routine traced its origins to a telephone call from Frank Hogenhuizen, proposing a dinner date. She was taken aback by the man's call, since she suspected Frank knew of her resentment towards him. She held him fully responsible for her husband's death. This, notwithstanding, the shameless man rang and said that he wanted to discuss a business proposition, a partnership.

"Frank," she said with all the patience she could muster, "if you are offering to sell part of House of Piet Snygrens to me just forget it. That store is ailing, and you should face your impending bankruptcy with dignity and courage. I will not put up a cent to bail you out of your financial doldrums!"

"I understand your sentiments," he said with uncharacteristic charm, "but I am offering something that is mutually beneficial to both of us. And to put the record straight, the finances of House of Piet Snygrens are solid. We have made impressive profits for the last three quarters and analysts are ecstatic about our performance and the future direction of the enterprise. We are easily out-performing our competitors, and there is no reason to suppose that trend will not continue for the foreseeable future."

She was unimpressed and shot back at him. "Don't take me for a rural third world woman. I am not totally ignorant … I do happen to subscribe to a newspaper, Frank."

"Oh, newspapers," he said sarcastically. "Now, you don't tell me that you would believe every single word written in *Rotterdam Weekly Herald*!"

"I don't read the crap in *Rotterdam Weekly Herald*. And anyway it is up to me to decide on the truth of what is written." She felt a strong urge to disconnect the line but nonetheless went on bravely, "I am talking about reputable newspapers. *Het Financieele Dagblad* and *NRC*."

"Quite," Frank said, as he sensed defeat. He hadn't wanted to prolong his agony. Indeed, House of Piet Snygrens was in financial woes, and the possibility of bankruptcy stared him in the face. The saving grace would be the securing of the three million euro to invest in the Thailand holiday resort that guaranteed to turn in an astronomical profit. The investment was a potential goldmine, Adrian Slangenveld had reassured. Within a short time, it would generate enough money to nurse all his other ailing business concerns back to health. Frank Hogenhuizen saw no reason to doubt Adrian Slangenveld's expert opinion. The challenge was to raise the money sooner than later. Upon his return from Thailand, he had gone to his bank, but the bastards had been unsympathetic. That is when he remembered that Inge Baleman-Ruyter had inherited large sums of money from Marc. If he could sweet talk Inge into entering a partnership, then his problems would be over. He knew the woman hated him, but there had to be ways to partner with people that detested his guts. He had discussed this with his bodyguard and right hand man, Joost Zwarts, who had brought him to a brilliant idea. Joost had pointed out that Inge was most likely a lonely woman. At this Frank had retorted impatiently that it didn't take a degree in psychology to come up with that unglamorous observation! He had little patience for people that stated the obvious. Smiling, Joost had pointed out that it was exactly for this very reason that she was vulnerable. "All you need to do is try to get her into bed, and she will bequeath all those millions to you!" The idea was charming in its simplicity, and in Frank's opinion, easy to execute. But he had to overcome the woman's hostility towards him.

"Be a lady! Do not dismiss me without giving me the benefit of ...," he had wanted to say "apologizing" which would suggest he was somehow admitting responsibility for her husband's death. However, he corrected himself in good time, "... give me the benefit of explaining, Inge. Do not behave like an overindulged schoolgirl, my dear lady! I am talking about a proposition that will make you dizzyingly rich, beyond what you and Marc ever entertained in your dreams. This is a chance of a lifetime, and I am making this offer to you only because I care so much about your welfare."

"I find this conversation quite revolting, utterly contemptible," Inge said. Pain and distress showed in her voice. "Please, leave me alone!" Inge screamed, as flames of righteous anger consumed her body.

"We could meet and discuss the proposal over dinner," Frank had insisted, determined not to let matters be. God knew that he desperately needed that money. "What do you say to *Park Heuvel* on Tuesday evening? They have a Michelin star and the food is a delight to the palate."

"No!" And an angry Inge had slammed down the phone, thinking, "What a disgusting man!" She wondered how Marc could ever have done business with such a thuggish insensitive man. Marc's loyalty to Frank had always puzzled her, and over time she had put it down to outright poor judgment of an overworked business executive. Or were they lovers? She shivered at that very thought, and she couldn't understand why it had to cross her mind.

Frank had stared at the dead phone in his hand and swore under his breath, "Bitch, you will be made to pay dearly."

———

Inge now lived in a state of trepidation, fearful of Frank Hogenhuizen. Given his shady business dealings, which were the subject of hushed conversation among the moneyed class of Rotterdam, Inge suspected that Frank would want to avenge the rejection and humiliation. She had a strong premonition that Frank was intent on harming her, ruining the life she had bravely and diligently built following the death of Marc and Rianne. After all, he had brought about her husband's demise, and could, at the drop of a hat, hire the services of a hit man to eliminate her. Inge had therefore telephoned her brother, Cees, a school rector in Arnhem, sharing her fears.

There was no doubt that Cees was a superb teacher with enough authority in his tone to awe a rowdy class of fifteen year olds into silence. Unfortunately, he was blissfully ignorant when it came to judging the ferociousness of men, for his belief in the goodness of humanity was deep and profound. Thus, he told his sister that she was overreacting. Privately, he thought that her nerves were early symptoms of an approaching depression, a rebound of the melancholy that had engulfed her in the past. Cees took more than a brotherly interest in his older sister; he considered it his duty, and especially after Marc's death, to protect Inge. But living in Arnhem as he did removed him from the responsibility of physically protecting her, and he had to contend with the regular telephone calls to Inge, calls in which his anxiety for her well-being were always prominent. She in turn appreciated her brother's show of loyalty, even if she frequently got put off by his patronizing attitude. If Cees had known of Frank Hogenhuizen's determination to get at Inge's money at any cost, he would undoubtedly have asked her to contact the police, and in that way an innocent life would have been saved. As it was, he advised her to have some rest and try to forget the matter.

"And girl, you can always come down here for a couple of days. Kitty would surely be glad to have you." Of course, Inge didn't doubt Kitty's unreserved readiness to have her in their terrace house. She had always got on well with her sister-in-law, a good natured saintly woman.

"Thanks for the invitation, Cees. I really prefer to stay at House of Java. Perhaps you are right. I am placing much significance to an inconsequential matter. I'll have some rest then." Inge thought of how lucky she was to have a caring and loving brother, a thought which led her to remember to show that she too cared about others. "I have a lunch appointment with Katrine during the week ... Friday."

Katrine was Cees' only child. Katrine had not been an easy child, and in her teens had chosen to associate with a group of antisocial youths that frequently had running battles with the police. She had dropped out of school at seventeen, and on turning eighteen, Katrine had stunned and hurt her parents with an announcement that she was going to cohabit with her twenty-four year old boyfriend, Jan Willem Beereboom. Two years later they were married. Family and friends had wished the couple matrimonial bliss, but unfortunately that marriage had not brought her happiness. Jan Willem was a prison guard, and he treated his wife as if she were a hardened criminal. He drank much and subjected Katrine to beatings at the slightest opportunity. In spite of repeated slaps and blows from Jan Willem, Katrine didn't see a need to leave him. She said she loved him and believed that over time, and especially when they had children, he would reform. Cees and Kitty had asked Inge to talk to her. Inge had advised her to stop the abuse by divorcing Jan Willem, arguing it would only get worse with time. The girl remained adamant in her conviction that her beloved husband was fundamentally a good man, which showed when he was not drinking.

"It is really kind of you to keep in touch with that young lady, sister. If there is anybody in the family she respects and listens to, then you are that one person. Any word of advice coming from either me or Kitty is suspect, tainted with the prejudice of old people. You have somehow found a way past her impervious unreason, and it does always work or at least makes her stop and think about her actions."

"Not always, though."

"Do you remember when she was experimenting with Ecstasy?"

Inge could remember that time alright. She had been called upon to talk to Katrine and had somehow managed to talk sense to her. Katrine had promised to stop with the practice forthwith, and she had surprisingly kept her word.

"Has she been around recently?" Inge asked.

"She was here two weeks ago."

"How is she doing?" Inge had not seen her niece for some time now. Although both lived in Rotterdam, Inge had never visited Katrine because she would not let her to. However, now and again, Inge invited her to come around, to visit House of Java. Most times, Katrine said she was too busy, preoccupied with one thing or other. Inge did not press her to visit, for Inge had a hectic life as well – pursuing hobbies and visiting friends.

"Same old Katrine ... still strong-headed, prone to making bad choices in life and madly in love with the prison guard! All the same do give her our regards."

Inge had accepted Cees' recommendation for bed rest and had kept indoors for much of the week. Her restlessness and distress at the impertinence of a man that she held responsible for her husband's death made it impossible for her to even contemplate standing at the window with the express purpose of sneaking a look at Uhuru. Although the disturbing telephone conversation with Frank Hogenhuizen still nagged her, she resolved to keep the Friday appointments. Besides, she was eager to do some shopping in city center. As she drove out of House of Java, the sight of Uhuru cheered her enormously, and she found herself forgetting Frank and filling her mind with thoughts of Uhuru, who earlier that morning had given her dizzying dozes of exhilarating pleasure, exhausting her with passionate numbness.

———

Inge drove to city center, left the car in the Grote Markt parking garage. She bought vegetables at the market and then walked to the butcher for boneless pork chops, sausage, and minced beef. It was not that she was any good at cooking, and she ate sparsely in spite of spending quite some bit of money on groceries which in most cases ended up in the garbage bin. She preferred going out to eat, and that was only possible when she had company. She wasn't in the habit of going to a restaurant alone. She was therefore hoping that with Uhuru at her side, they could freely walk in and out of restaurants.

As Inge walked in the Beurstraverse, she saw a particularly flirtatious black dress on display in Helen of Troy, a high end lady's boutique store. She had a strong urge to expand her wardrobe with the fashion of youth. She considered stepping in and owning that dress for Uhuru's benefit because she convinced herself he would surely approve. However, she was tempered by her legendary indecisiveness which might take her a good part of an hour before making up her mind to buy a dress. She therefore decided to defer buying it to another occasion when she had more time on her hands. She didn't want to be late for the eleven o'clock meeting with her manicurist. Then she was to meet her niece, Katrine Beereboom, at *De Harmonie*, for lunch.

When Inge had rung Katrine to make the lunch appointment, Katrine had surprised her by mentioning that she had found employment as a shop assistant at House of Piet Snygrens. Of course Katrine was unaware of Inge's ongoing rancor and distrust towards the proprietor of House of Snygrens. Anyway, Inge reasoned, on one hand her niece reserved the right to choose her employer without undue influence from an overbearing widowed aunt, well-meaning in her intentions as she may be. This consideration notwithstanding, Inge perceived that her niece was now working for her sworn enemy, fully on the payroll of an adversary that had destroyed her husband's life and denied her happiness. She had no intentions of telling Katrine what she thought of Frank, but nonetheless she would try to encourage her to look for alternative employment, a resolve that had increased in the light of Frank's insulting telephone call. At the same time, she realized it was not an easy matter trying to change Katrine's course of action once her mind had been made up. Katrine was obstinate by nature and unyielding as a matter of habit.

Inge doubted if a short time at House of Snygrens was enough for Katrine to develop strong loyalty with the fashion house. She therefore thought the task of convincing Katrine to abandon House of Snygrens wouldn't be difficult. She would offer to help her get a better paying job. Perhaps she could interest her in setting out on her own, perhaps a nail beauty salon in the very heart of Rotterdam. Of course, Inge had her doubts about Katrine's readiness to invest time in acquiring a pedicurist's diploma. Nonetheless, Inge convinced herself that the girl would not resist a magnanimous offer from her aunt.

———

When they had finished their lunch and were having a cup of coffee, Inge tentatively explored ways of leading Katrine away from House of Snygrens.

"What are the prospects of a permanent appointment at House of Snygrens?" Inge asked in a well-practiced tone of pretended interest.

"I should secure that without a problem," Katrine said confidently. "As it is I had a chat yesterday with Erik Hooymans … that is our line manager. He was full of compliments. He said I have picked up much faster than any new girl he has ever known. And Erik should know … he has been in the business for a pretty long time."

"How sweet, Katrine!" Inge exclaimed, rather too enthusiastically. "I only hope the rumors about House of Piet Snygrens aren't true." She observed a bluish-brown blotch on Katrine's left forearm and winced inside. She was reminded of Katrine's broken nose the previous year, some few days after Easter. Poor girl, she thought. Why don't you report that unfeeling husband of yours to the police? Inge pretended as if she hadn't seen the blotches. However, she was brewing with anger and resentment underneath the external façade of civility. She understood what it meant to be battered by a coercive and manipulative husband. Inge had had her share of domestic violence. It was her first marriage, which had lasted two horrifying years. He was a stock broker, a perfectly ordinary fellow with a disarming smile to the outside world, but a violent terror, a near psychopath, at home. Each time he slapped or raped her, he said he regretted his actions and would never touch her again. Each time she believed him and said she was willing to give him a chance, just this once. The final straw had come when at the height of an angry tantrum, he had thrown a cup of scalding coffee on her lap that resulted in hospitalization and treatment for second degree burns.

"What rumors, Aunt Inge?" Katrine asked, rather taken aback. She laid her cup of coffee on the table and put her hand over her half-open mouth.

"Financial troubles, girl. Impending bankruptcy possibly." Inge watched Katrine's discomfort.

"Oh, Aunt Inge! Does that mean they will be laying people off and things?" Katrine saw her world of financial security collapse around her.

Inge shrugged her shoulders, sipped her coffee thoughtfully and said, "Who knows? These things do happen rather frequently. Companies file bankruptcy and folks have to look for other things to do. This is not a good moment to have bankruptcies. The economy is unusually soft."

"I was only recruited recently, and I can't believe they offered me a job when they knew the company was struggling and soon to close!" Katrine suppressed a spurt of anger, before sighing heavily and shaking her head, "It is unfair, Aunt Inge. They should have told me right at the outset that the place was going bust. I would then have looked for something else!"

"Ah, you are still young, which presents you with lots of opportunities," Inge ventured, vigorously stirring her coffee.

"That does not give them the right to treat me like this!"

"Remember these are rumors, my dear," Inge said in a soothing tone. "All the same, if I were you, I would start thinking ahead, looking elsewhere. One needs to be one step ahead of the pack, if you know what I mean."

Katrine was overwhelmed with desperation. "What shall I do now?"

Inge smiled, and it was a toothy smile of self-satisfaction. "I'll see what can be done. Perhaps you can set out on your own. After all your line manager seems to think you have the aptitude, and I am sure you have the determination to succeed." She hadn't imagined it would be this easy to convince the girl. If only she could manage to convince Uhuru this easily, then she was out to have great fun, Inge reflected.

"My own thing?" Katrine asked in a tone that was at once total disbelief and welcome relief. "Well, it is not like I have lots of money, but I will see what we can do for you."

Then Inge had mentioned the nail beauty salon. "Of course some effort from your side will be required. Studying for the diploma shouldn't be hard. You will need that piece of paper before city officials allow you to touch people's toes. There are correspondence courses all over the place, and the good thing is you can start anytime and at your own pace. You will need to give it your best shot though. If you are to succeed, you must quit the job and concentrate on the study. Needless to mention, I'll support you financially for the period that you will be pursuing the pedicure diploma. If I were you, I would start immediately. Think about it, Katrine."

"Fantastic, Aunt Inge!" Katrine said in a voice overflowing with new optimism. She knew that her aunt's riches were legendary but never before had she been the recipient of her magnanimity in such overwhelming abundance. That act of generosity brought tears into her eyes, and she half-stood, leaned across the table, and affectionately kissed her aunt's cheek.

Inge paid the bill, leaving behind a generous tip for the young waitress. Outside, a street surveillance camera circling above them, she reminded Katrine to tender in her resignation as soon as possible. Katrine said she would do that within a week. Then Inge, satisfied with the success of her lunch appointment, left for Noordwijk aan Zee.

———

Inge and Annemarie walked on the sandy Noordwijk aan Zee beach in spite of the overcast sky and faint mist, which explained why there weren't many people up and about. Erozan had been admitted at the clinic for observation. Understandably, Annemarie found it all too distressful but for Erozan's benefit had grudgingly agreed to leave her in the care of the vet. After fussing about the dog for a good three quarters of an hour, Inge steered the conversation to the subject of her visit, resisting the temptation to discuss her golf putting skills. Annemarie listened to Inge's account of Uhuru with disbelief and extraordinary elation.

"He has this thing about him ... I mean ...," Inge stammered as she struggled to find appropriate words to describe Uhuru's effect upon her. She momentarily stopped, and everything about her seemed so insignificant. Inge was oblivious to the roar of the sea and the strong wind that rustled about her legs. Only Uhuru was alive in her mind, pulsating in her heart. Then lightening up like a candle flame since dismissed for dead, she found the words that had eluded her. "He has such a sweet and civilized manner. Uhuru's face and laughter do give me this virginal impression of being young once again and ready to celebrate life with unrestricted happiness."

Annemarie observed that at the mere mention of Uhuru's name, Inge's eyes twinkled with the naughtiness of a woman on a blind date with an attractive and witty gentleman. Inge, always reserved, so proper, thinking of getting a young lover! And a tall, broad-shouldered black man at that!

"Seems to me you can't go on without him," Annemarie said with deep conviction.

"I long for him with the violent intensity I once craved for Belgian bonbons. Remember that period?" Inge said with unlimited delight.

Annemarie could remember alright. It must have been a decade or so ago when Inge gravitated to all things sweet, and the Belgian bonbons were her breakfast, lunch, and dinner. The extra kilos were evident in all the wrong places! It had taken her months of hard work following a strict dietary regimen before she could shed off the excessive redundant fat.

"You are in love, my dear. I suspected it all along!" Annemarie triumphantly bent to pick a stick, which she threw far into the distance out of habit. But there was no dog to run after the stick.

"When did you realize that?" Inge asked, blushing in spite of herself.

"During my birthday. The glitter and vibrancy in your eyes did you in. I certainly knew you had met that someone special, a gentleman far better than our Henk Koopmans. I can't wait to see him, Inge. And I make a solemn promise: I won't grab him from you!"

The women laughed, and for once Inge was thankful for the cool, screaming, salty wind that permeated her body, diffusing into her inner self, invigorating a spirit deep in love, and precipitating her thoughts into a sensual terrain uncharted for many years. She talked endearingly about her love, and asked Annemarie as to how best she should express her feelings to Uhuru, for it was a long, long time when she was last in love. She found it amusing that she, at an age when she should be contemplating hormone replacement therapy, should be engaged in thinking up elaborate plans to ensnare a young black man.

"Invite him for a glass of scotch and tell him how you feel about him." Annemarie broke into spasms of excitement. She was reminded of that dark night in the Gambia, drinking whiskey with a young black man. He was a waiter at the four-star hotel where she and Paul were staying. She had wanted to have him the first time she had laid eyes upon his ebony skin. It hadn't been difficult to get him in bed, in fact he was all too eager, and his indefatigable performance had not disappointed her.

"Isn't that being too brazen?" Inge had thought that she had given Uhuru enough hints about how she desired him. Somehow she believed that with time, he might get the message. She was sure he had almost overcome his inhibition the previous week at the roadside park. She wouldn't rush him, she decided.

"Not in the least, my dear! It is what I would do if I were to be confronted with a similar situation. And believe me there is no better way breaking the ice of a budding romance over a scotch. Let the young stallion know you are in love, and the rest will follow."

"But suppose he rejects me? I wouldn't stand that!"

"That is irresponsible rationality!" Annemarie said sharply, "Why would he reject you? Is it because he is married or something?"

Inge nodded, impatiently pushed a curl out of her eye and said, "That and also the fact that he might not be keen on an older woman who could be his mother's age." She didn't know how she would cope with the humiliation of a rebuff. But she didn't imagine that Uhuru would not find her desirable. Nonetheless, the very contemplation of a remote possibility of rejection made her feel insecure. Perhaps she should accept that an affair with Uhuru wouldn't amount to much given their disparate ages and different cultures, and their diametrically opposed stations in life. He was a married man, seemingly a loving husband and caring father. Perhaps, she reflected, it was much better to just adopt him in the certainty that he would be there for her to pamper and nurture with maternal love. But then, try as she might, she failed to see in Uhuru a foster child. All that she clearly saw was a man that she wanted to shower with love of a carnal nature.

"My goodness," Annemarie exclaimed, "you talk as if you are the most senior of the inhabitants of a nursing home, and the ugliest of the lot at that! You aren't a hideous looking elderly woman, Inge. You are middle-aged and good looking, always have been. Fifty-somethings have a right to some fun! God knows, I deserve a merry time, too!"

Inge allowed herself the luxury of a smile. For she, too, was determined that age shouldn't be unfairly used to keep her away from Uhuru, and she was glad Annemarie shared the sentiment.

"The people around me … friends …," Inge hesitated.

She had wondered if love was justification enough to suffer the risk of social ostracism. Inge was acutely aware that her community did not hold ethnic minorities in high esteem. Since employing Uhuru, she had taken a keen interest in the so called "ethnic minority question," and she now felt that Uhuru and those like him were being unfairly targeted when people tried to explain the failings of an individualistic society indulged by decadent consumption. Yes, she had appreciated in the last few days the systematically choreographed subtle language of bigotry portraying ethnic minorities as dangerous by instinct and outright subversive by natural inclination. And it surprised her greatly that she had read and heard this harsh verdict in the past without stopping to consider its merits. Would her other friends unreservedly welcome Uhuru? Was she woman enough to ignore moral bounds, so to speak, take a decisive step and walk away from the condemning and disapproving eye of public opinion? Or would she be making a fool of herself? There were the high class ladies of the golf club to think about as well. The club boasted of one non-white, a Japanese businessman. Would they view Uhuru as a kind of Tiger Woods or would they look at him as a primitive intruder, a Johnny-come-lately that has to be grudgingly tolerated? She decided to be perfectly subversive, devilishly defiant, and to pursue her interests irrespective of what others might think.

"Let your conscience decide and not the prejudicial weight of public opinion. If our ancestors had been prejudicial, we would probably still be Neanderthals!" Annemarie pronounced emphatically.

Inge was strengthened by Annemarie's open and liberal attitude. "I am okay with the conscience part of it. You are yet to tell me how I should go about winning Uhuru's heart. I need an unambiguous roadmap, if you see what I am driving at."

Annemarie grinned and winked her left eye. "I would make it clear to this Uhuru that his continued employment depends on a willingness to have an affair. Period."

"You are suggesting blackmail?" Inge said with ignoble outrage. For all her being in love with Uhuru there was still some degree of maternal benevolence she felt towards the young African. She found Annemarie's proposal insensitive. She would not take advantage of her superior status as a woman of immense wealth to force Uhuru into an affair. She wanted something mutual, a relationship built on trust and respect and not one that based its legitimacy on abuse of power. There was no question of her exploiting his insecurity. Be as it may, she desperately and almost violently desired to possess him. Inge wanted exclusive rights over Uhuru, and for a second or two felt a pang of indignant jealousy, a momentary touch of intense hatred for that other woman in Africa. However, upon quick reflection that she had no right to be hard on Uhuru's legal wife, she felt a sense of mortification and softened a bit.

"Well," Annemarie said positively ghoulish, "you asked for advice and you got it." The remark was concluded with a laugh and shrug. Then there was momentary silence as the women walked on the sandy beach. They passed a man sweeping the sand with a metal detector in the hope of finding some rare coins or antique metallic objects of great monetary value and not the usual mundane buttons and buckles of recent holiday makers. A young couple, hand in hand, sauntered past them. About ten meters away the couple stopped, laughed with the gusto of youth and kissed passionately. Seagulls circled above the water and in the distance two dredgers, as if sandwiched between the end of the blue sea and the beginning of the gray sky, almost imperceptibly bobbed on the waves. Inge kicked the sand in front of her, and for the umpteenth time Annemarie bent to pick up a stick. But this time round, Annemarie threw the stick into the roaring waves of the North Sea. With nothing else to talk about in the matter of Uhuru, Annemarie grumbled about how she missed Erozan, and Inge advised her to seriously consider joining the golf club. "It is fun, you know," Inge said.

Having no other urgent tasks to perform at House of Java for the day, Uhuru gathered the tools of his new trade, a green Black & Decker grass mower, rake, hedge shears, and wheelbarrow into the large tool shed that he had initially mistaken for a guest wing. When he arrived in city center he sought out a telephone booth; he had to get hold of Mirembe, explain why he hadn't rang Mapenzi. The very thought that he had not kept his part of the bargain caused him tremendous unease and he felt like a traitor. He dialed and waited, but the phone rang for long without being picked up. He looked at his watch. It was five-thirty. "That is six-thirty in Uganda," he thought sadly, his spirits sinking like the six-thirty Ugandan sun disappearing behind distant hills. Without prior arrangement, it would have been lucky if he had found anyone in the office at such a late hour. Uhuru weighed his options, and realized that short of requesting Inge for an afternoon off, he might not be able to get his message across to Mapenzi. He was still assailed by a sense of fear for his job, somehow believing that if he requested for an afternoon off in these early days of his employment Inge might misconstrue this as laziness and lack of interest in the job. Uhuru was acutely aware of charges of laziness that were leveled at immigrants, and he didn't want to give anybody an excuse for firing him on that score. Resigned, he made his way to the public library where he divided his time between gardening books and his old passion of reading Dutch history and society. The focus of his current intellectual pursuit was Johan van Oldenbarnevelt, the founder of Europe's first trading republic, and one in whose boundaries, hundreds of years later, Uhuru found himself, etching a living in an environment more hostile, he supposed, than the eighty years war. He was reading Jan and Annie Romein's book on Dutch history. He turned to a page that he had read several times and read those words he had committed to memory, the chilling sentence of one of his heroes, van Oldenbarnevelt, a man that had held high office in Rotterdam, Uhuru's city:

May Thirteenth, 1619. The Hague. The *Binnenhof.* The scaffold erected the night before. The sand. "Your sentence is read, come forth, come forth." The executioner. The seventy-one-year-old man, his upper body naked - "no, milord, the other side, so you have the sun in your face" - the last sun and the last words to the people there: "Men, believe not that I am a traitor. I acted upright and godly as a good patriot and so shall I die," the very last words at the very last sunlight, to the executioner: "Make it short, make it short." A swishing glint, a dull thud, three or four fountains of warm, dark, living human blood. And it is done.

After reading this account he briefly considered the cruelty of life in the low lands. He happily noted that even if the law were to catch up with him, because of illegal stay in the country, his fate would be far better than that of van Oldenbarnevelt. At best, he reflected, they would take him to a holding center, that angst eliciting gulag in the polder, before unceremoniously deporting him with a stern warning not to attempt sneaking back into the country. He put a logical spin to this thought; he wouldn't be the first to be banished from the country, for far worthier people, such as Hugo de Groot, were banished from the Netherlands.

Fifty minutes later, Uhuru left the library, crossed the street, and walked towards the tram stop. He passed a man juggling a can of coins at passers-by. The hapless wretch was evidently a homeless junkie whose hollow-cheeked sallow face and grizzled beard was a disquieting disharmony of unkemptness. Uhuru, just like the multitudes in the busy street, hurried past without bothering to stop and part with a coin. But this man, in terminal stages of decomposition, wasn't taking this disinterest gracefully, fretting and cursing as if pedestrians were duty-bound to give him alms. Uhuru was just in time to hop onto a full tram that gave him a sensation of being trampled underfoot. He remained standing till two stops further down the road when a seat became vacant. He rushed for a seat by the window, and with a nod invited an elderly woman to take up the unoccupied space beside him. But the woman who had been standing with only fragility to keep her balance on a clattering tram forcefully declined to take up the offer. In fact, as soon as Uhuru's eyes locked with the sour expression in her fading blue eyes, she hurriedly looked away, tightening her grip on her bag before pushing forward through the tangle of bodies crammed in the aisle. Was it mockery or contempt? He imagined it was both. But what was it that made him such an object of undisguised hostility? Uhuru wondered in surrender. It was a question he had posed to himself countless times whenever he rode the tram or sat in a train. Anyway, over time, he had learned to put up with the frequent disillusion of rejection and to accept that most people in this country were ill at ease with his company, his illegality, notwithstanding. The bona fide residents of the country seemed to go out of their way to avoid him. He thought of that saleswoman at House of Snygrens. Perhaps she had thought he was a swindler or a misogynist or even something worse – a rapist, murderer? How he would have loved to show her otherwise! But again, the prejudice was so widespread that the most effective way of countering stereotypic thinking was to embark on educating the entire community, a task, he felt, far beyond his capabilities. Uhuru admired and envied the likes of Abraham Kuyper, Baruch Spinoza, and, yes, his hero, van Oldenbarnevelt, for their courage to stand up, defend a philosophy, and change a people's way of looking at things. If only he were as gifted, he would have written a long treatise to the *NRC*, *Trouw*, and *de Volkskrant* arguing that ethnic minorities, whatever their legal status, were not profiteers in this country. They were not here to sponge on free social benefits. That was not their primary reason, not their motivation. He would have stressed that ethnic minorities must certainly not be viewed as a group keen to drive western civilization to a state of barbaric depravity or third world destitution; they were as eager as the next man and woman to participate in building and maintaining a prosperous society based on equal rights for all and respect for the rule of law. But that desire to excel was systematically thwarted which led many to instinctively fight to survive by any means. No, they were not benefit cheats, and the country ought to realize and acknowledge that, and not go on as if they didn't trust them not to defecate in their splendid backyards. Amadu had once explained to him why it was that his race was so despised in Europe, "Now and then, a man needs to identify himself above the filth of mankind, to elevate his thoughts and actions to a position of superiority. Good friend, we as a race serve a useful purpose in that vain, human game. We are thus used as receptacles into which these crass men and women spit venomous words that belittle and reduce us to a race of morons so that their own sense of moral and intellectual superiority is both perpetuated and enhanced."

Uhuru looked out of the window, beyond the cars driving on the cobble stoned street next to the tram and beyond the milling crowds on the wide pavements, and turned his attention to the large windows of the cozy red brick walled houses. A few windows had lace curtains but most had curtains pulled back. It was surprising that the sight of these windows brought upon him a sense of profound nostalgia, a gnawing homesickness. He remembered telling Mapenzi about windows on Dutch homes, and she had been immensely fascinated by the fact that one could look right into the living room.

"I would hate people spying on me, Uhuru!"

"My dear, Mapenzi," he said, "ours is not a police state!" He wanted to add but didn't say, "Even if we are in perpetual fear of the police, eager to hunt us down as rats during the plague."

"But just imagine, no sense of privacy." Mapenzi was alarmed.

"Well, there is no sense of shame to begin with. You could walk about nude in your living room, and it would attract nobody's attention, believe me! How about stripping nude and

119

sunbathing on the sandy shores of Kralingse plas? It is a spectacle I see every summer."

That was too much idiocy for Mapenzi, and she said that she was sure he was trying to pull her leg. She thought he was using the term "nude" metaphorically, although she couldn't work out the metaphor, and there wasn't enough time to ask for an explanation. He said he was hanging up in two minutes time, and for some inexplicable reason, he had an urge to know if Watoto Inc. was still in business, a discussion that consumed the last of the fifteen minutes of their telephone conversation.

The bleak entrance of the Prof. A.S. van Vredeman block and the musty air of the lift contrasted sharply with the sweet expensive scent of wealth within the walls of House of Java. Uhuru closed his eyes briefly, inhaled deeply in the hope of reacquainting himself with the intoxicating essence of Inge's perfume, whose scent was essentially aphrodisiac. As he stepped out of the lift, he was surprised to see the House of Snygrens' shop assistant. He hesitated for a moment before saying "hello". And without as much as looking at Uhuru, she mumbled something unintelligible back, avoided the lift, and sauntered away in aimless haste. She either doesn't remember me or if she does, then she has done her best pretending not to have noticed me, Uhuru reflected. Did she live in the apartment or was she visiting? Letting her fade into insignificance, he walked along the long corridor to number 741 E, struggling with the question that had preoccupied him for some time now.

Uhuru had vacillated for a long time as to whether to confide in Greg and Pierre about Inge. Yes, they were friends, and finding himself so far from his homeland, he had come to consider them as family. Should he tell them about the suspicions that were gnawing at his heart and producing a trance of troubled thoughts? Uhuru had a growing feeling that Inge fancied him. That ride in the car, the stop at the roadside park, and the look of longing she had given him when they sat side-by-side on the bench. Is it possible he had imagined that face which begged to be loved? He decided to share his thoughts that were at once fact and doubt with Pierre and Greg. Of course, there was no question in his mind that even if his suspicions were true, he would not betray Mapenzi and Juliana. But these were mere thoughts which were divorced from his feelings. And yet Uhuru had to admit his infatuation with Inge—the lovely face which though of an older woman retained a deliciously mischievous spark of youth and the heaving rounded mounds of desire revealed the outline of firm nipples that gave her an irresistible attractiveness. To Uhuru, Inge's beauty was agonizingly desirable. The thought of his big black lips, cracked by the humid wind, kissing her delicate pencil-line lips sent his body alight with carnal curiosity, a desire to explore further territory. He had to make a conscious effort to banish these feelings that had not spared him, even in his dreams. On one occasion, two nights past, he had had to wake up and change into clean pajama shorts. He didn't feel embarrassed about it. It was a rather pleasant experience which he would have liked repeated outside the realm of dreams.

When Uhuru entered the apartment, he found his housemates in animated conversation. There was Alisi, Amadu, and Washington Keya for company.

"Ah, there enters the proletariat!" Amadu said cheerfully.

Uhuru smiled. "Nice to see you folks. Have you been around for long?"

"I've been around like for a week," Alisi said with cheek. There was laughter.

"Dropped in together with Amadu about half an hour ago," Washington Keya said.

"Our neighbor is dead," Greg said unceremoniously, as though he was making a casual observation about the spring weather.

"What!" Uhuru screamed.

"Apparently a massive coronary," Pierre said. "He collapsed in the bathroom, and it was too late by the time the ambulance came around."

121

"Wait a second!" Uhuru said, sounding alarmed. "Which neighbor … 739 or 743?"

"739," said Alisi.

"The old man with the dog?" Uhuru asked. He had never had the opportunity to talk to the deceased man, and that hurt him. He found it almost weird that he had lived next to the deceased man without as much as saying a word to him. It would never happen in the countryside where he grew up. Out there avoiding social intercourse was regarded as uncivilized, the zenith of poor upbringing and an uncontested manifestation of boorishness.

"The one and the same," Greg said.

Uhuru sought unequivocal confirmation from his friends, for there were a few old men in their apartment block with dogs. "Are we talking about the man with the golden retriever?"

"It is not a golden retriever," Greg said in a tone of one that knew much about dogs in spite of having never owned a pet. The dog in question was a Saint Bernard, a fact to which Greg was evidently oblivious.

"Whatever it is," Alisi interjected, "its owner is dead."

"But I saw him yesterday, alive!" Uhuru said.

"My dear man," Amadu said, "You can't die today unless you were alive yesterday! And that is even not philosophy or rocket science as they are apt to say these days." He sounded rather amused, like a schoolteacher correcting a child who adamantly insisted that two plus two added to three because that is what his father, a prominent and respected lawyer, had said.

"And should you think of going for the funeral then just forget it," Washington Keya said. "Funerals here are not an affair for the entire village like back home."

"By invitation only," Alisi said.

Washington Keya shook his head. "Outright strange, isn't it? Nonetheless, not stranger than what we have just witnessed outside, in your parking bay."

"Not another one dead, I pray!" Uhuru said and sat down for the first time since entering into the room.

"No," Washington Keya assured. "I was just telling the others about this rich Surinamese man, the one with the BMW."

"Yes, guy at number 427," Uhuru said. Just like most people living in the apartment, he knew Fred Bos was the black man with the red, sexy, two-seater BMW Z3. It was said he had some important position with a multinational company, and beyond that Uhuru and his friends didn't inquire. Nonetheless, it was gratifying to see that a man of color could live in such comfort, something that gave them hope. But they had never understood why he didn't move out of this derelict apartment block to pitch tent in the desirable and affluent neighborhood of Kralingen or Hillegersberg. Pierre insisted it was all about the Dutch culture of penny pinching, something Fred Bos excelled in. It was rumored he had no girl, never touched alcohol, and had never offered anyone a free drink. In other words, Fred Bos was your quintessential niggardly Dutchman.

"He was in the car parking bay engaged in a scuffle with the police," said Amadu, as he took over from Washington Keya. In subdued silence and incomprehension, Uhuru listened to Amadu narrate how police, acting on a tip off from a resident in the apartment block, had come in full force to investigate Fred Bos' source of income. They wanted him to explain how it was that he could afford an expensive car when the police borough chief, a hard-working man with over twenty-five years of service on the force, could not afford even a pre-owned BMW.

"They were working on a couple of false assumptions," Washington Keya said.

"A couple of assumptions?" Greg sneered. "Let's call a spade a spade and put an end to our tendency to skirt around a painful subject, just because it makes us aware of our unwelcome in this country."

"Are you suggesting he was singled out by the police because he is black?" Uhuru asked.

"I can swear to that," Greg nodded.

"No fucking cop came to interrogate any of you. You know why? You are all black dudes owning crappy second-hand cars, which cough and sneeze in the winter. Ethnic minorities parking expensive cars in underprivileged neighborhoods are suspect! It is official, dudes," Washington Keya said.

"What happened eventually?" Uhuru asked.

"He was so furious that he kicked one of the policemen, a black man like himself, trying to grab him by the scruff of his neck, as if he were a common criminal," Amadu said and shook his head. "And that did it! They overpowered him, and he was bundled into a police car. He knew he had done nothing wrong, and it was foolish of him to lose his temper."

There was so much frustration in the room at the shared realization of victimization, and the men clicked their tongues in rage and shook their heads in defeat.

Alisi made effort to reintroduce gaiety in the room. She asked if anyone cared for a drink, and all the men chorused almost simultaneously that they were dying of thirst. But on second thought, Greg declared he would have preferred an early dinner before settling down to a drink. Unanimity being not uncommon, the others also found Greg's idea appealing. Alisi said she was not in the mood to cook anything substantial, and that they would have to make do with a simple meal, white rice and *Sambal Goreng Telon.*

Amadu's mouth was watering. "Whatever that is, Alisi?"

"Egg in hot *sambal* sauce. I am sure you would like it."

"Of course, Amadu likes everything!" Greg said and laughed.

"Not true," Amadu protested. "Grasshoppers aren't my thing, turns my stomach."

"I would give everything for grasshoppers fried in butter," Uhuru said.

"I am off to the kitchen," Alisi rose up from the sofa. "It will be *Sambal Goreng Telon* and not grasshoppers. I hope I am not disappointing someone."

When Alisi was gone, Pierre said he had new *soukous* music CDs that he wanted the others to listen to. So there was loud music and laughter as Alisi busied herself in the kitchen.

In the past weeks, Uhuru had refrained from volunteering more information about his employer beyond saying she was kind and that she was appreciative of his work. Now, in this relaxed atmosphere, he saw an opportunity to put a question that had been nagging him to an audience of self-proclaimed experts on all things Dutch. He asked Pierre to turn the stereo volume low, and then told them about his day with Inge at the roadside park and other suggestive gestures that Inge had displayed towards him, on more than one occasion. They were spellbound as Uhuru recounted his tale. "Is she making romantic overtures or am I misunderstanding the entire situation?" Uhuru asked.

"She is giving you all kinds of leads, my friend," Pierre said in amazement at Uhuru's idiocy.

"That woman is looking for a good shag, begging for that timid thing dangling uselessly between your arthritic legs, can't you see," Greg said and clicked his tongue in disapproval at the way Uhuru was letting a golden chance slip out of his fingers. Greg had made it a point to drive his ramshackle Volvo 360 past House of Java. He had taken Washington Keya with him. The two men had gawked at the massive mansion in wondrous amazement. Washington Keya had remarked that if the next military coup succeeded (he still had contacts with young soldiers yearning for a change of government, eager to kick out the long-serving despotic ruler), and he became president, he would build his presidential mansion along the architectural plans of House of Java. It would have to be even bigger, he had said. The men had left Kralingen fully convinced that Uhuru's employer was not just another wealthy person, but that she was a multimillionaire and probably with lots of influence. Greg almost wished it were him doing that gardener job, which, if truth be known, he had despised in the beginning. But after that visit to Kralingen, he was in a better position to appreciate the silver lining that lurked behind every cloud.

"Imbecile of the first degree!" Amadu the poet ejaculated.

"What a timid and blind chap you are," Washington Keya confirmed, as he placed a hand on Uhuru's arm.

125

"Trying to play the fidelity game with that Mapenzi of yours!" Pierre said. "You could be rich. Think about that dude! Stinking rich, eh!"

"Volkswagen Touareg!" Amadu said and licked his lips, as if the car were a thing to eat like the delicious *Sambal Goreng Telon* that Alisi was cooking for them.

"Off-road gray," Greg said and blinked rapidly, visualizing himself behind the steering wheel of this power house on wheels, luxuriously cruising from Maastricht to Groningen. "Soon, she will trust you enough to allow you to clean the Touareg, and with time entrust you with the car keys. Shag that woman dude!"

Uhuru shook his head in defiance of his friends' ludicrous suggestions. "I will not take advantage of Inge's loneliness."

"I quite don't see your point," Pierre said.

"Anyway," Uhuru persisted, "like I have already said, I will not do anything that will hurt Mapenzi or Inge for that matter."

Greg laughed contemptuously. "Hurting Mapenzi! Anybody ever heard of this magnitude of sheer stupidity?"

"I say," Amadu said with controlled patience, "you hurt her more with your puritanical obstinacy. Think of the bags of money you would be able to send to Mapenzi. Think of all those nice things that you would be able to afford for your beautiful daughter."

"And the residency permit that she would undoubtedly give to you! Think about yourself, raised above the rubble of obscurity to a respectable status of the moneyed gentry," Greg said.

Amadu assented rather loudly. "Yes, dude, you lay her good, and that elusive residency permit is yours on a silver plate! People like that Inge of yours have contacts. She must have influence with the big-wigs that make immigration policy. Yeah, the ones whose goal in life is to keep third world destitutes like us out of Europe. A telephone call to the right people at the Immigration and Naturalization Department or to our beefy-faced mayor, and the people that matter will go on their knees, begging you to accept the residency permit … even Dutch nationality and perhaps a job driving that she-devil of a minister of

Alien Affairs and Ethnic Minority Integration! No exaggeration here, but that is a generous payment for a lay! I say, I have yet to meet a man as lucky as Uhuru!"

"Haven't you guys got a conscience, no sense of shame at all? Have you all taken leave of civility and the rules of common decency?" Uhuru asked. He regretted telling them about Inge.

———

If Uhuru had foreseen this careless and unfocused volubility from his mates, it would have been better if he had worked out a scheme in total silence, he thought with a twang of regret. Hearing these men urging him for reasons other than feelings of love for Inge flew in his face, and he was outraged. He wasn't a mercenary type, the kind of folk that looked for a Dutch partner for reasons that weren't entirely noble.

There was a discreditable chap he knew. He had married a Dutch girl, a pretty young morsel with a freckled face, for reasons of getting a residency permit. Upon receiving his residency permit, he had been decent enough not to show his wanton greed immediately, postponing it for one year. But in the process, they had been blessed with a child that he now looked at as a curse, an impediment to a carefree lifestyle of weekend partying in dingy Amsterdam neighborhoods and regular visits to street prostitutes. For occasionally, this perfidious fellow was called upon by his ex-wife to baby-sit, which invariably and inevitably interrupted his pleasures leading him to screaming out profanities at the mother of his baby. Uhuru despised such callousness, and he had genuinely believed that most of his friends would harbor similar sentiments. When his friends emphasized the material aspect of a relationship with Inge, at the expense of strong feelings of mutual love and respect, he was assailed with disillusion in the honesty of these men he had come to consider as family. How dare they, to treat Inge as if she was one of those drug-addicted common whores hanging out at Rotterdam central station or the infamous Keileweg Street? The whole thing was immortally insulting and immeasurably disgusting! How he had bundled up with this batch of material-minded mercenaries was beyond him.

"You want to talk about human conscience, Uhuru? Listen, dude, and listen carefully. The destitute have nothing and are willing to sell their conscience, soul, and all in return for something to keep them afloat on this turbulent sea of deprivation and hardship," Amadu said with biting mockery

"Well," Uhuru said and shrugged his shoulders with finality, "I've got to think of Mapenzi and Juliana. Both are the reason I continue living in this rough neighborhood, among unreasonable so-called friends. Can't you all get it? I love Mapenzi!"

"She might be married, for all we know!" Greg said, as he laughed sarcastically. "Take the widow, dude!"

"I will do nothing of the sort," Uhuru said with convincing resolve. "I am a man of high moral principles, and I have no intention of exploiting a lonely woman. It isn't right, can't you see?"

"But what is right in this country?" Amadu asked, bemused.

"Yes," Pierre acknowledged, "what is right about capitalism? It is all about making money, and it is quite irrelevant to dwell on the means of how one goes about making a quick buck. If some rich widow is the conduit to a trove of treasures, so be it!"

"Thou shall not walk away from a gold mine," Washington Keya declared, as if he was giving commands of no retreat to rebel army officers on the eve of a planned military coup.

"That is for me to decide," Uhuru said and drew a deep breath. He could not bear this gross vulgarity anymore. And with swift agility, he rose up and exited from this unbearable situation. As he closed his bedroom door behind him, he could hear amused laughter in the living room and someone remarking that the beauty of his principles was in their inconsistency. They could laugh for eternity if that is what suited them, reflected Uhuru moodily; their laughter could not erase his sense of honor to the two women that cared so much about him and whom he respected. As he plopped down on his bed, he was struck by the absurdity of not having seen his wife in as many years.

Chapter 6 Mutual love

Annemarie stood beside Inge, observing Uhuru go about his tasks in the garden. Annemarie had wanted to look at him in all quiet, without betraying to Uhuru that two pairs of female eyes were focused on his body, mentally undressing him and reveling in his nakedness.

"What a handsome and shapely *neger*!" Annemarie declared breathlessly, impressed by Uhuru's dashing, healthy, and strong features. "I must admit he has a pleasant, honest face."

"He is such a dear," Inge said with pride, "extremely decent and rather well-mannered."

"It is hard to imagine he grew up in the bush-bush. When you read the newspapers nowadays, they tend to paint them as if they are Satan's first cousins! Look at him … he is such a *lekker ding*!" And in her mind, Annemarie now felt the powerful hands of another young black man, as they lustfully clutched a handful of dimpled fat loosely hanging on her bottom, grinding a massive blackness into her moistness and sending her to scream with a pleasure that she had never imagined could be associated with such an act. The Gambia! Now that she was divorced, she should think of going there again, possibly this coming winter. Perhaps I could get Inge and her black boyfriend to come along, Annemarie thought excitedly.

"My very impression the first day I set eyes upon him," Inge said proudly. "*Lekker ding*, worth serving after a delicious dinner."

"I can now see your total lack of interest in our Henk Koopmans," Annemarie winked with carnal significance. "There is more man in our *neger* than in that overweight and balding Henk. I envy your choice, girl!"

"Thank you, Annemarie. But he is still not mine."

After observing him for a good five minutes trimming the hedge, close to the gate, Annemarie declared that he reminded her of someone famous, although she couldn't quite figure it out.

Uhuru's shirt came to Inge's mind. "Not Mandela, I suppose."

"Not Mandela but ...." Annemarie concentrated hard.

"Then who?" Inge was extremely curious.

After a minute or so of deep concentration Annemarie exploded with the excitement of discovery: "Denzel Washington, of course!"

Inge too began seeing the similarity. "Sure! I should have thought of that one myself!"

Indeed, if Uhuru were to overhear their conversation he wouldn't have been entirely surprised. He had heard it often enough. Some white folks he had informally encountered in the streets or super market had remarked about his Eddy Murphy looks, and yet others swore by the dykes that hold back the North Sea that he was the twin brother of Umbataka, a hulking black soccer player with the unglamorous looks of an insane bulldog but nonetheless gifted with quick legs that instinctively knew how to safely deposit a ball in the net. He had long come to the conclusion that to white Dutch eyes all black people were indistinguishable, and not only their physical appearance but their entire character.

"I was thinking," Annemarie said.

"Yes?"

"He is too sweet to share. I would die of jealousy knowing that I am sharing him with another woman."

"I shan't be sharing him with anybody!" Inge said with resolve.

"No? I recall you saying he is married!"

"All right," Inge admitted, then as an afterthought, "That is if you can still refer to two people that haven't seen each other in more than six solid years as man and wife. Does that sound like marriage to you?"

"Well, you do have a point about that one, my dear. All the same you should discuss with him about divorcing his wife."

"Why would I do that?"

"Because you love him and want to have his black cock to yourself."

"Not his cock, Annemarie ... at least that is not the primary thing." Inge said with a tone of voice sounding decidedly upset.

"So what is primary?"

"His love, of course!"

"The two are one and the same thing to me, anyway."

Before Annemarie left House of Java, she jokingly remarked to Inge that if she was slow about getting this young man to bed, then she should consider sending him over to Noordwijk aan Zee. And when Inge playfully said she was hell bent on taking her man, Annemarie declared with all the innocence in the world that all she would ask him to do was to wash the window glasses of her villa and nothing more. "But if he finds window washing a rather hackneyed tiring exercise I wouldn't mind suggesting something more challenging! And believe me I would not go about him with your slowness and patience."

"Meaning what?" Inge asked, laughing.

"I would invite him to be quick about undressing me!" Annemarie's eyes welled up with mischievousness, and Inge bent over in laughter.

⸺

Uhuru, dressed in his gardening denim overalls, had been working for some weeks now at House of Java when on a sunny April morning he was delightfully surprised by Inge's presence in the flower-scented garden. She didn't come down often. Inge had just finished talking to Annemarie on the telephone, and she had again, as on countless other occasions talked excitedly about possibly being irrevocably in love with Uhuru. Annemarie had strongly advised her to make haste and put an immediate end to the emotional torment.

"He looks so cuddly, dear!" Inge had said.

"Oh, a warm and tender teddy bear!" Annemarie laughed.

"True indeed," Inge had pronounced, "I could hug him all day long!"

"Declare your true intentions to Uhuru, sweetheart," Annemarie had said and sighed resignedly at her friend's indecisiveness.

Thus propelled into adapting a more brazen approach by Annemarie's persistent encouragement, Inge had gone to her wardrobe and stood there a long time, undecided on the right form of outfit that would look casual and yet inviting to someone as young as Uhuru. She didn't want her dress to appear like a premeditated gesture laden with naughty libidinousness, but rather as something she had slipped into because it happened to stare back when the wardrobe doors were opened. She finally made a choice, dressed, and stood staring in the full-length mirror for a long time, as she alternately studied the dress and her face, giving particular attention to the delicate narrow nose, the one that Marc found so enchanting and her parents said was inherited from her maternal grandmother, a woman of profound charm and wit. She ran a hand through her hair, pulled at her shirt to straighten a crease, pushed up her breasts and turned to peer at her back. The image in the mirror convinced Inge that in spite of her age she still had an appeal and didn't doubt her ability to make a lasting impression on a young man. And yet, she wasn't sure if Uhuru would see the same image that stared back at her. She felt inadequately equipped to guess what it was that might appeal to an African man, for she had hitherto never had occasion to reflect on such topics. She now mused that she didn't have the slightest clue on how other cultures perceived sex. Perhaps there were cultures where men hurriedly dismounted halfway through an orgasm, ran to the fridge for a quick bite on a hamburger! She laughed at her cheek and said loudly to herself, "Naughty girl, Inge! Put an end to the fantasies!"

In the bathroom, Inge applied grey eye shadow and pink lipstick. Then she sat on a straw chair, put both feet on a low stool, and painted her toe nails a bright red color. When she had finished painting the toenails of her left foot, she put it off the stool and stepped on the tile floor. The warmness of the travertine tile floor was soothing, like the caress of a man's hand. When she was done and the paint had been given ample time to dry, she slipped her pretty feet into green suede slides. She now had to get the ideal perfume that could stand up for the occasion. There were numerous bottles of expensive perfume in the bathroom cabinet, and for a moment, she didn't know what to pick. She settled for a sensual and intimate Paleis OrgasExotika. She applied the perfume to her wrists, crook of her arms, nape of the neck, and her cleavage. One final look in the mirror confirmed that she was ready to take on Uhuru, to put an end to a long period of procrastination. She hurried downstairs and was soon in the garden. She waved to her unsuspecting quarry saying, "Ah, my workaholic! What about a tea break?"

"Thanks, Inge." Uhuru carefully put down the watering can as he turned to face her.

Inge was wearing white Capri trousers that rustled softly in the morning breeze, and with mischievous recklessness, she had the top two buttons of her blue shirt open to reveal a white silk bra. The shirt she had knotted just above the belly-button. Uhuru hadn't seen her looking so desirable and so refreshingly young. And the scent of OrgasExotika sent titillations of pleasure down his spine, settling in the area of his crotch. He found her gorgeousness at once desirable and intimidating. He dropped his eyes to conceal his confusion, but then his face momentarily lit up at the sight of those delicate toes painted red.

Sensing his uncertainty, she said with delight, "Must I come and carry you, sweet heart?" She then laughed, and her laughter was infectious and totally liberating, freeing the inhibition within him. But in the same breath, Inge's presence had resurfaced a vague guilt within Uhuru. He was confronted with his own naked lustful glance that he had greedily displayed when the two of them had snuggled close to each other on the park bench. Now, her inviting attitude led him to relax, and he joined in her laughter, laughing with that carefree manner that seems to be patented by Africans. And his head swirled at those endearing words, "sweet heart", which kept coming back again and again, like the courtship duet of birds on verge of mating. Had she uttered those sweet words from the bottom of her heart or was it merely a manner of speech she used when addressing her friends and acquaintances or even worse, her gardeners?

"I'll just finish with this flower."

Inge half-playfully wagged her right index finger at Uhuru. "You love the flowers more than the lady of the house, eh, naughty boy?" She hoped this message was clear, and if not she was willing to get bolder, break what she perceived as his childlike indecisiveness. Or was he just naturally shy?

Later, they sat at the kitchen table, facing each other. Uhuru slowly munched a cookie as he listened to Inge talking about her plans for the summer holiday, occasionally brushing crumbs off his overalls. Inge talked about previous summers, all very glorious and refreshing. She said she enjoyed making acquaintance with other cultures. Operas, museums, cathedrals, palaces, Roman ruins, and the like, she said. She wondered if the renovation work on the Sacre-Coeur was now over. Last time round it had been one mess of construction work in Paris, she excitedly said. And last summer, she had been to Portugal, Algarve, with Annemarie and Paul. Wonderful golf courses in the Algarve, she said. Then she said they should think of enrolling Uhuru at her local golf club because he struck her as one with a natural instinct to hit the ball long and hard. Then she drifted away from golfing, a subject that was so dear to her heart, Uhuru perceived. Inge said she now had plans to spend time in Corsica but she had not made up her mind yet. "There are those fires that seem to happen every summer," she complained. "I don't fancy seeing myself caught up in the middle of a relentless blaze. I dislike knowingly walking into a disaster which is certain to ruin my vacation." Then she wanted to know if Uhuru had made any definite plans for the summer vacation. If not, she added, they could go off together.

"I have never found it necessary to go on vacation," he said truthfully. In fact he never understood what the entire fuss was all about; travel trailers and camper vans grid locking highways, as the annual summer vacation pilgrimage painstakingly snaked its way southwards to the warmer climes. Back home vacation was in December, around Christmas time, when townsfolk left the crowded towns for five days of festivity with their countryside kin and kith. He had even heard of some officials with well-paying jobs who were dead scared of taking even those five days of rest, in the belief that in their absence some upstart might maneuver himself into their position, making it a top priority to go through the files, exposing financial shenanigans of phenomenal proportions.

Now Inge was suggesting he could accompany her on holiday! He couldn't believe his luck! As much as he might have wanted to accompany her on vacation, he realized that his freedom of movement was curtailed. He could not risk traveling outside the Netherlands and was even weary of leaving Rotterdam. He must disappoint her, he reflected. Uhuru thought that revealing his illegitimacy in the country would lead Inge to fire him, a deep fear that walked with him day in, day out.

"If you aren't keen on Corsica, we could settle for the south of Spain or France ... somewhere coastal," Inge said dreamily. "Do you like the beach, Uhuru?" Her voice dripped with excitement as she visualized Uhuru in tanga briefs (she was sure his crotch was not a mere superfluous decoration, and that it would excite ninety percent of the women on the beach, assuming the remaining ten percent had a natural disinclination towards men), a barrel of a naked chest with a golden chain, glistening muscular biceps, lying next to her in black skimpy pants. She enjoyed sunbathing topless, and she visualized herself thus on a pristine beach beside Uhuru, pale skin tanned to a healthy golden brown. Then she saw them visiting one of those discos found in places where tourists flock to, discos where there was no distinction between old and young. They would dance the salsa or even an energetic African tribal dance if that was Uhuru's fancy. In a moment of reflection, she had to concede she didn't dance the salsa but she was confident Uhuru would teach her, after all he was young and had to be familiar with the beats and steps of the youth. Maybe she should already ask him to teach her the salsa, she thought. She had always wanted to learn the salsa and now looked forward to dancing the summer night away like a professional, shaming the more seasoned Latin girl who might be on the floor. She did not stop to consider that Uhuru might be unable to dance the salsa, that he might possibly be one hopeless fellow when it came to any form of dancing, including rhythmic African dances. She just had this intuitive thing that all Africans were good dancers, a kind of in-born thing that one invariably acquired with the dark skin. Uhuru, she sighed discretely, you have transformed my life and made it worth living!

"Yes, I do like the beach. But I am not good at swimming." Uhuru had only been to the pristine sandy beach of Scheveningen on two occasions. His confession about his lack of swimming skills embarrassed him profoundly.

"Didn't you get swimming instructions as a child, in elementary school?" Inge asked with sympathetic interest and a benign smile. She was not exactly put off by Uhuru's inability to swim. On the contrary, it would come in handy since they would then spend most of the time lying under the parasol and in between sipping Piña Coladas caressing each other.

This question almost sent Uhuru laughing. In the village where he grew up, nobody ever had time to think about organizing swimming classes for children. There were more important things to worry about, such as the failed crops, lack of money to send the children back to school, or where to get money to buy medicines for a sick child. Uhuru told Inge that indeed there were no swimming classes on offer in his village. "Anyway," Uhuru said, "I could waddle in the sea and lie in the sun. But there is …"

"You are coming, then!" Inge declared triumphantly, not willing to listen to his stupid excuses. This time round she was more than emboldened to have him, and she was determined to be in full control of this conversation. She stood up, walked round the table and planted her lips on Uhuru's cheek.

"It is awfully ... awfully kind of you," Uhuru stammered as Inge gave him another kiss on the cheek, "... awfully kind to invite me, madam." How could he tell her that her offer was well-appreciated but due to a cascade of circumstances outside his sphere of influence, and in fact beyond the reach of anybody that he knew, he could not accompany her? Inge was now placing a delicate pale hand on his strong well-rounded shoulders. If it had been intended as an affectionate touch then it should have remained in that position for a very brief moment and more importantly, that hand would not have begun to caress Uhuru. The lid was coming off Inge's long-standing self-imposed inhibition that had, she was sure before this encounter, turned her into a frigid widow. Desire and an intense flare of longing left her helplessly tired that she found herself sitting on Uhuru's laps. She knew she was getting blood in her cheeks but she didn't allow this to distract her present enterprise; she would carry it through to its joyful end (for she believed it couldn't have any other ending). She had to take charge, be responsible for guiding him. Inge was determined to show him all her affection. Yes, she was going to show him her love that was far deeper than a naked desire for a man just for the sake of comfort, for satiating a base need. Inge fingered Uhuru's ebony skin with the absorbing intensity she reserved for her own body when standing under a hot shower. Uhuru was at first shocked and at a loss for what might be required of him. As Inge proceeded with the intricate sensual circling and rubbing movements of her hands all over his body, Uhuru found himself rather enjoying it. Poor lonely woman! Uhuru thought. Is she in love with me, an illegal alien? True, he hadn't been candid in relating with her. He should have told her right at the very beginning that he was an illegal alien. But wouldn't that have denied him the job that he so much wanted? He had to support Mapenzi, Juliana, and more recently he had got a letter from his sister saying that they could no longer afford the insulin that kept her nine-year-old diabetic daughter alive. She had pleaded with him to send some money, twenty euro. Pity had stirred his heart, and he had promised himself that he would send a check of fifty euro to his sister, as soon as he got his wages. "Poor lonely woman!" he again thought of Inge as she feverishly started unbuttoning the top buttons of his overalls and running a hand trembling with passion on his bare chest. It is at this point that sympathy must have flown into passion, and Uhuru was seized with a maddening sentimentality that pushed him into the grips of love. Thus, jumping out of his inertia and discarding indifference, he tightened his arms around Inge's fragile waist, hungry lips feverishly kissing her neck with a forcefulness that momentarily took Inge by surprise.

"Uhuru," she whispered with tender charm, heart pounding with passion and body aching with unfulfilled desire to love and be loved. She squeezed her delicate body against his as if her intention was to blend into him, to become one body afire with passion. Feeling the firmness of his arms tightening harder around her waist, she lifted her eyes to him, in total surrender to his embrace.

"Inge," he said and looked lovingly into eyes that were at once inviting and pleading. He didn't know what to say next without coming across as clumsy and unnatural. So he just tightened his arms around her waist and pulled her closer to him.

She looked at Uhuru indulgently and flashed him with a disarming smile. "I have always loved you. I love you, my sweetheart, Uhuru." How she had wanted to say those words! Now that the pertinent words had been uttered, she was assailed with a feeling of relief like one finally attaining release after an unbearably long period of hesitancy at the edge of orgasmic rapture. Her happiness was profound, and it was as though she was inhaling new life. She was in high spirits as Uhuru gathered her into his arms, stood up, and carried her to the sofa in the living room. He gently lowered her on to the large red sofa, and on his knees started to fidget with the knot of her shirt. She half-rose, to assist him undress her for she couldn't wait anymore. "Do you love me, Uhuru?" she asked since she was yet to hear the reciprocal words of endearment.

"Inge, I …," Uhuru started, a tingling sense of excitement in his throat. But the shrill sound of the telephone stopped him in his tracks, suspended the unspoken words of undying love that stood frozen on his trembling lips.

"We are ignoring the phone," Inge commanded, breasts heaving with ecstatic breathing. But then she thought it might be something urgent, perhaps her niece Katrine in grave danger. "*Verdorie*," she cursed the phone. She asked Uhuru to bring the headset to her. It was Frank Hogenhuizen.

"Am I interrupting?" Frank asked slyly.

The miserly man couldn't leave her in peace, she thought bitterly. Frank again proposed dinner. Inge had to name any restaurant of her choice, Frank said. But Inge was not impressed, and she told him to dismiss any ideas he entertained about her. There would be no meeting between them. She didn't want to see him, ever. He pleaded for a chance, just one chance.

"This evening, then? Please!" Frank hated pleading with this woman.

"Fully booked and unavailable, sorry," Inge said with merciless impatience. She looked at Uhuru who for lack of anything adventurous to explore was now inspecting her bookshelf. He picked up a book from the shelf, leafed through it and not finding it good enough to engage him for more than a fraction of a second, carefully placed it back.

"What are you doing?" Frank asked.

"It has never occurred to me that I must justify my actions before you," she said, as anger begun taking a better part of her. The high-pitched angry tone of her voice forced Uhuru to stiffen, the leather-bound book in his hands suddenly as heavy as a wheelbarrow full of sand. For hitherto he had associated Inge with gentleness, a woman without a trace of temper. As Inge continued the heated exchange, Uhuru wondered if it was anything that had to do with him. He thought of quietly slipping out of the house and returning to his digs, for he was aware

Inge's conversation with the party on the phone was never intended for him to hear. But then another thought, rather disturbing, occurred to him. Suppose Inge was being threatened by some violent madman? Then it would be callous cowardice to beat a hurried run, leaving her all on her own. Now was the time to show her he cared, a moment to stand by her side and lend emotional support. Yes, he loved the woman! But he also loved Mapenzi. Why had he allowed himself to be caught in such an intricate web of divided loyalties? How could he best save himself, redeem his credibility as a husband and father without hurting the feelings of an older woman he had grown to respect and was now in love with?

He heard Inge saying on the phone, "Well, if you insist on knowing … I do have a lover, and we are going out tonight, to dinner." And with those concluding remarks, she disconnected Frank.

"That is Frank Hogenhuizen …," Inge said in way of explanation to Uhuru. She was remarkably composed and gentle for one that had just been agonizingly angry. "I think I previously told you about him. He is out to have my money, and heaven knows what he is capable of doing to reach his goal. Now, we are going to forget him. He shouldn't be allowed to stand in way of happiness. Uhuru, you and I are going out to dine. No, no," she said on observing Uhuru's face gearing up to launch some flimsy excuse, "I most certainly will not entertain your protests. Now that is settled, and you can go home now. I expect to see you around at six o'clock." And that was a command.

Later that evening Inge introduced Uhuru to the luxuries of affluent living, the little pleasures and indulgencies of the moneyed society. She had reserved a table at *Klomp & Tulip*, a trendy, upscale market restaurant just outside Capelle aan den Ijssel. It was a quiet place where diners were of such civilized and polite manners that they hardly looked in the direction of a young black man walking into the restaurant, hand-in-hand with a middle-aged white woman. Uhuru's presence in *Klomp*

& Tulip barely caused a stir. The food here was of a rich delicateness that even Alisi, good cook that she was, couldn't match. It almost sent him bursting out with laughter, thinking of what his housemates might be eating at that very moment since Alisi and Latasha were spending a week with Milagros in her Delft apartment. Tinned fibrous asparagus harvested years ago, as if they had no idea spring was the season for fresh asparagus! There would probably be some fish fingers and spaghetti, which was easy to boil. As much as Greg and Pierre would have preferred rice, they had yet to learn how not to boil it to pap. Uhuru fared better at cooking, and whenever Alisi wasn't in, they begged him to cook for them. But that was their apartment, and he had to concentrate on the present which found him here, in *Klomp & Tulip* dining amongst Holland's plutocrats, the privileged class unscathed by the economic malaise.

—

Uhuru and Inge had had the wild Nile bass with a red mullet farce and were enjoying their dessert surrounded by a palpable iridescence of candlelight. It had been difficult for Uhuru to choose anything from the incomprehensible leather-bound menu card, and the outrageous prices made the pleasurable experience of eating fine food rather uncomfortable. For he continuously looked at the prices in the light of the suffering back home. Before Uhuru had met Inge, he would not even have brought himself to fantasize dining in this exquisitely pricey establishment, and the truth of the matter was that he did not imagine such places existed. But now he sat back in his cozy chair with the airs of one who had known luxury all his life, and it was his second nature dining in establishments of this caliber. He even found himself unconsciously scratching his cheek, and not because it was itching, but rather to display the luxuriousness of a rich carefree life in the manner of rich, but incoherent sportsmen during a prime-time television interview. The sheer chutzpah of it all surprised him, and soon his thoughts turned to his poor village kin and kith. They were perhaps retiring to bed without dinner, and yet here he was being dined like royalty! He reflected briefly on the injustice of unequal distribution of wealth and opportunities. He was shocked to see this other side of the affluent world, more so for one whose ideas of "dining out" were limited to exotic restaurants frequented chiefly by immigrants or to Big Mac and a large size milkshake in the event that he tried out mainstream cuisine. But he didn't dwell much on the subject, lest it got between him and his appetite, for Uhuru enjoyed good food. The South African white wine (it was a Chardonnay, from one of the oldest and finest vineyards in Stellenbosch Inge had excitedly declared, praising it's wonderful aroma with an off dry finish on the palate) to accompany the fish had been brought at a cost of fifty euro, the exact sum he had promised to send to his sister to save her diabetic child.

Inge turned her spoon playfully in her rhubarb soufflé. Uhuru noted that she ate very little of the expensive food, she had just nibbled at the delicious fish whilst Uhuru had seen no reason to show modesty. For he believed that if one paid so much, then one had to have more than his fill, tuck in as much food till one was on the brink of nausea. What good did it serve to just nibble at a fish here and a salad there? He remembered the last time round when he was at McDonalds with Pierre. Pierre had declared that he wasn't going to finish his sandwich, and Uhuru had happily picked it from him, finishing the sandwich in four big greedy bites. But in *Klomp & Tulip*, Uhuru was determined not to create an impression of an uncultured tribesman just emerged from the frontiers of the African savannah, some godforsaken place where famine ruled supreme. The rules in *Klomp & Tulip* were definitely different, and that much he could recognize. This chic restaurant was not a rendezvous point for the working class, a crowd at home in an outfit celebrated in Pierre Kartner's *Het kleine café aan de haven*, a lowlands classic, a roaring anthem for the inebriated proletariat.

Inge encouraged him to try some exotic sounding dessert that was outlandishly expensive … more than the price he had paid for the Dockers trouser he was wearing. He had declined, choosing something familiar instead. Vanilla ice cream. The entire meal, he would note later with something close to alarm, cost Inge far more than what he paid Greg in rent every month. It was evident Inge, wearing a seductive black lace cocktail dress, was in her element here, among her social equals, although not necessarily like-minded since he was the only alien in the place, save for one or two waiters. Indonesian ancestry, he presumed. Then his mind wandered to Watoto Inc. that Mapenzi had said was now a restaurant. He visualized the shouted orders and harassed looks of waiters, as they hurried about slumping plates full of steaming bananas or goat meat on tables possibly laden with flies. The contrast was too big to contemplate, and yet, he surmised, the food may be equally good albeit different.

Uhuru and Inge chatted and laughter flowed effortlessly between them. Inge told him about her childhood dreams of working somewhere in the third world. She had always been keen on development work, helping the poor to climb out of misery, treat sick children and ailing pregnant mothers, providing clean water, and more of that sort of humanitarian work. "I did admire Mother Theresa of Calcutta," she said and laughed as she sipped wine. Uhuru said he thought Mother Theresa had done a wonderful job, caring for the destitute. He said he was sure there were lots of Mother Theresas out there in the wider world, many unrecognized. He said he knew of a kindly Ugandan woman who had opened up an orphanage, looking after children that had lost both parents to war or AIDS. Moved by tales of orphans, Inge said she was frightfully sorry for all those "little miserable black souls." Then he changed tact, gradually and craftily leading her away from grinding destitution. He reminisced about Ugandan cuisine, stewed groundnut sauce, roasted goat meat, and green plantain (this reminded him of a singing Mapenzi, sitting on a mat, knife in hand, peeling green plantains at an amazing speed). Inge listened with fascination, looking into those large black lively eyes that she found thrillingly provocative.

"Don't you miss your traditional food?" Inge asked with sincere solicitude. She scooped up the rhubarb soufflé, upturned it, and proceeded to flatten it in the plate in a movement reminiscent of a pathologist meticulously rubbing a cervical smear on to a microscope slide.

"Sometimes." He finished his ice cream.

"What would you say is the typical African dish that you miss most?"

Uhuru did not bate an eyelid. "Frozen elephant balls, and they are my favorite any day."

"Sounds divine to me!" she enthused. "Spiced?"

"Very spiced. Hot, like in chili pepper."

"That, sweetie, is a hundred percent testosterone diet! How do you get hold of it?"

"Needn't look far really. Every self-respecting *Toko* store, where ethnic foods are in abundance, has enough stock to go around."

"Please do promise that you will someday cook elephant balls for me." Inge pushed the rhubarb soufflé around the flat plate. Uhuru put his hand under the table, and gently stroked Inge's thigh. They looked at each other and laughed.

"Oh, you are such a wild savage, you're a primitive beast!" she said with mock annoyance.

They laughed loudly as the candle flames flickered gloriously, filling the restaurant with a luminous yellowness that tranquilized their minds. The atmosphere brought to Uhuru the image of the mellow interior of a Buddhist temple in Thailand. He knew about Buddha temples only from postcards in his student days. A fork fell out of the hand of an elegantly dressed woman at a table to Uhuru's left. But before her husband, for Uhuru assumed that the man seated with her had to be the husband, could retrieve it from the floor, a waiter materialized from nowhere. He picked up the fork and within no time he was back with a clean one, all rolled up in a massive white cotton cloth napkin. Uhuru and Inge were silent for a minute or two, the fallen fork having taken the center of attention and distracted them somewhat.

"Tell me, Uhuru," Inge said seriously.

"Yes?" Uhuru reached for the glass of wine.

"What is your opinion about women?" she asked, holding her left hand to Uhuru. He didn't hesitate anymore but reached out and took her warm hand.

"The loveliest humans ever to be created." Uhuru was enjoying the banter.

"I don't mean that," Inge said with genuine seriousness etched on her furrowed forehead. "Wife beating and that kind of thing ... that is what I want to know." Inge had read that most ethnic minorities in the country held women in low-esteem, and wife-beating was an accepted norm. This was one aspect where she still had reservations about her relationship with Uhuru, and any man for that matter.

"Wife beating?" Uhuru echoed, a distinct consternation on his face. "Now who in his right mind would want to beat his wife, or any other person for that matter?"

"Look, I am awfully sorry," Inge said, as contrition got the better part of her. She bent over the table and laid a hand on his arm and smiled reassuringly. "It is just that one reads so much about these things. Ethnic minorities that and ethnic minorities this; all quite negative, I promise you. It is all too confusing, and one doesn't know how best to shift wheat from the chaff."

A moment of silence followed before Inge turned to unfinished business. "I am so glad we are going on summer holiday together."

Now, thought Uhuru, *is the hour of reckoning. I must tell her, and if she chooses to fire me that is her prerogative.* Uhuru fidgeted about in the chair, impatiently rubbed what had now become his imaginary itch on the cheeks. Unlike cheek-scratching, moneyed soccer professionals or famous actors, there would be no deliberate stammer but the telling of the absolute truth, even if that meant the death knell for his prospects as a gardener. This could very well be the end of hobnobbing with Inge, but so be it. He waited for the coffee, which was brought by an extremely polite waiter dressed in a fine black pinstriped vest, white shirt, and black bow tie. Uhuru made his confession in the fading echo of the waiter's retreating footsteps on the well-polished oak floor.

"I am an illegal alien." Uhuru cast his eyes down in embarrassment. He could see what had until now been a cozy evening coming to a tragic end, an anticlimax in which he would be accused of betrayal and deceit, with the inevitable termination of employment.

"So what?" Inge said.

The evening's excitement was slightly deflated by Uhuru's confession. She had heard and read much about illegal aliens and asylum seekers drowning the place, but she had considered the entire discussion as abysmally trivial, something that could hardly impact on her life. And when Gerda, an enthusiastic golfer and wife of the managing director of a multinational transport company, went on hunger strike in protest at what she saw as violent and inhumane treatment of unaccompanied minor asylum seekers that were hermetically isolated from the rest of the Dutch society at a camp in the south of the country, Inge had problems comprehending her drastic actions and even thought her claims of brutalization rather exaggerated. She made it sound as if the campus was a concentration camp, which Inge believed couldn't be true. On another occasion, Gerda, in her characteristic way as the flag bearer of the underprivileged and downtrodden, had tried to recruit sympathy for the unaccompanied minor asylum seekers among the ladies of the golf club. She had, on verge of hysteria, appealed to her fellow golfers to sign a petition to the parliament to dismantle the unaccompanied minor asylum seekers' camps, which, in her opinion, flew in the face of all that was decent and civilized. Most of the women, including Inge, had refused to sign the letter, not because they were in support of government policy, but more out of indifference and a desire to distance themselves from issues that bore little relevance to their lives. Inge had followed the rise of Fortuynism and other variants of right wing populist politics in the country with detached amusement, like one watching a bad soap for lack of anything more entertaining

146

or engaging on television. She viewed the culture of growing intolerance towards anything alien as an episodic, temporary phenomenon with roots in the country's history. Every generation of self-respecting Dutchmen had been ingenious in creating and isolating a marginal group, subsequently blaming their failures on the hapless defenseless people. In her times, she reasoned, the alien now occupied that unenviable position, a punching bag on which to aim all the country's frustrations and fears. The more she had thought about the alien question in the last weeks, the more she was convinced that much of the generalizations about the dangers posed by aliens boiled down to centuries of deliberate ignorance.

"I can't travel outside this country," Uhuru said dispirited.

"But you do have a passport, I suppose."

"Yes," Uhuru managed to stammer, cup of coffee suspended midway in apparent confusion. The dim glow of the candles that a while ago symbolized the ultimate romantic environment, now cast grotesque shadows of damp emptiness in his head, and he felt a strong urge to put the flames out, to end this derangement.

"Then, I don't see the problem," Inge said, after a moment of reflection.

"It is like this," Uhuru began, embarrassed uncertainty in his tone, "I do not have a residency permit. I am staying illegally in this country, the Kingdom of the Netherlands. If I am caught, then it is deportation for me ... detained and airlifted back to Africa. I can't travel to France with you or anybody else. I can go nowhere in Europe for that matter ... I am a *persona non grata*. Inge, I am so sorry to have caused you such distress and grief. I should have told you right from the beginning, but I needed that job ...," he blinked rapidly to hold back the tears of emotion that threatened to come flowing out like the irrepressible waters of the Nile rushing to the Mediterranean Sea, "... I desperately had to find a job. My wife, my daughter and countless relatives ... all of them are counting on me to fend for them. I have deliberately not told you about my sister and her diabetic child … Oh, God, what have I done to you Inge! I take responsibility for this mess and beg your forgiveness, madam."

"Oh, do lift yourself up!" Inge was touched by his eloquent speech and, at the same time, acutely made aware that he was married and had a daughter. But in spite of this knowledge she could hardly bring herself to think the thought of losing Uhuru. It would be an injustice to have him torn away from her, and she was not going to sit idly by and watch Uhuru living in perpetual agony of deportation. How she loathed the very thought! She refused to accept that his illegality meant that her love for him was illicit. Not at all put out by the weight of the country's law in the matter of aliens and not giving much thought to the political ideology of xenophobes or other bigots and demagogues, she confidently declared, "Nobody is talking of firing you. In fact, I do not see any wrong you have committed. Why should anybody stop you from living here? What right do they have? What right did we have colonizing Indonesia and all those other territories? You belong here, Uhuru, just like me!"

They drank their coffee in an uncomfortable silence that was broken by Inge's determined voice swearing with forceful certainty, "I'll see to it that you stay legally in this country. Whatever it takes!"

"Aren't you cross and disappointed in me?" Uhuru asked.

"For goodness sake, Uhuru! I do love you." She took his hand again and squeezed it hard.

"You are a wonderfully sympathetic lady." The shadow of uncertainty lifted from Uhuru's face. It was times like this that one identified a true friend. "I'll be indebted to your kindness forever." He reached for the bottle of wine. But before he could get to it the waiter, mannerisms groomed to indulge the wealthy, materialized from beyond the soft glare of candlelight, swiftly but gently taking upon himself the happy and honored responsibility of taking charge of the wine bottle. Uhuru nodded his appreciation as the younger man poured wine into his glass. The waiter inquired if the lady wanted wine, as well. Inge politely declined, adding that she was driving. With something like a curtsy to both of them, esteemed and privileged clientele, the waiter retreated back into invisibility.

At a quarter past eleven, Inge paid the bill and insisted on dropping Uhuru off at his apartment. In spite of his feeble protests, her will was done. Finally, the Volkswagen Touareg turned into Uhuru's street. They kissed in the car parking bay, and the smooch was more complete and passionate than earlier in the day at House of Java. Her heart beat unevenly with the recklessness of the moment as her wet tongue, with urgent eagerness, tenderly explored the sensual darkness of his mouth, licking away the bruise of a harsh reality of his illegality. And in a sweeping movement Uhuru ran his hands through Inge's blonde hair as if he were brushing away the lethargy that had settled on their minds that evening. She in turn whispered soothing words to comfort him, looking at him adoringly, taking evident pride being in his presence.

Inge's eyes twinkled. "You could stay the night at my place, you know."

"It is very kind and considerate of you. But I've got to go. My housemates might get worried and ring the police. Besides you are leaving for Rome tomorrow."

"Yes, Rome will be one depressing city without you, Uhuru."

Before Uhuru had come into her life, she had looked forward to the long weekend in Rome with Annemarie, escaping the festivities and fuss around Queen's Day. But now she hated that separation from Uhuru, even if it were for a few days. Anyhow, it was a four-day trip that she and Annemarie had planned last autumn, and she considered it a breach of trust, a betrayal of shared confidences if she were to announce to Annemarie that she was canceling the trip. There was such a thing as loyalty, she concluded. She would not allow selfishness stand in the way of a long and treasured relationship. She would go to Rome and make the best of it, she resolved.

The eternal sound of cars driving in and out of the parking bay, slamming of car doors, and laughter from happy inebriated people returning to the apartment after a night out in Rotterdam reminded her that Uhuru had reached his destination and would have to leave the car. "You don't have to go now … I mean right away," Inge whispered. "You will stay a little longer in the car, won't you?"

Uhuru smiled and nodded his head. "I will stay in the car for as long as you want me to." He leaned over and kissed her again, and it was invariably exhilarating exploring each other inside the car. Inge encouraged Uhuru to explore her breasts as she took liberty to feel his crotch. She wanted him to take her then and there, on the back seat of the car like a homeless couple with no other decent place to retreat to for a moment of shared intimacy. But she was conscious that would violate the rules of common decency. For all the recklessness of being in love, she was still a dignified woman. The sex would have to wait for another time. Important things, like resolving his stay in the country, had to be given precedence, and the rest would follow. Inge stole a glance at her Tank Louis Cartier watch. It was more than one hour since they had left *Klomp & Tulip*. Their sense of perception had been dulled by tongues exploring mouths, busy hands venturing to and squeezing delightful territories. Time had marched on without their full participation, outside their conscience. She realized that they couldn't stay in the parking bay all night, as much as the moments of shared intimacy were perfectly satisfying.

"See you next week then," she whispered to Uhuru.

"Sleep well, Inge."

Inge remained in the car parking bay, watching him walk to the apartment block. At the entrance, Uhuru stopped. He turned to face the Volkswagen Touareg and waved spiritedly. She waved back, gave him a flying kiss, and then headed to House of Java. Stopping for a red traffic light, it occurred to her how empty her house was. How had she managed for this long alone? Wouldn't it be exhilarating and liberating to have a man in her home again? She felt a need to return to the agreeable comfort of domesticity. She had enough resources to take care of both of them, so he needn't have to worry on that score.

Uhuru's stay in this country had to be legalized, she resolved for the umpteenth time. She knew that as long as he remained in illegality, their love would have to be lived clandestinely. She convinced herself she would work towards legalizing his stay, not necessarily out of ulterior and selfish motives of claiming him for herself, but rather out of a desire to correct an injustice. Surely, he had been in this country for some years now, spoke the language (and she had heard or read, much to her surprise, that Dutch was among the world's most difficult languages only rivaled by Basque and Finnish, and Chinese did not come even close!), was keen to work, and had not engaged in activities that could be described as dangerous or subversive to the wellbeing of the Dutch society. She wanted him to be a free man, unchained from the yoke and stigma of unwanted alien, liberated from the constant angst of imprisonment and deportation. Maneuvering the car into the Kralingse Plaslaan, she allowed an outline of a faint smile that remained long enough on her lips to cause a chuckle, as she thought about how deeply in love she was with Uhuru. As she turned left at the roundabout, she felt energy drain out of her, and she was all of a sudden tired and sleepy. She sighed. She couldn't wait to get in the Treca de Paris bed and dream about her Uhuru.

Chapter 7 The demise of illegality

Inge tossed and turned in her bed, thinking of how to rescue Uhuru. Uncertainty suffused itself in her mind, and she wasn't sure on how best to proceed. Common sense told her that she would have to solicit for advice. That she was traveling to Rome with Annemarie in the morning had a purgative effect. Annemarie was apt to know the best way forward, and she would ask her to solve this one. It was just that Annemarie seemed to understand how the Dutch system worked, no doubt knowledge learned from a world-wise Paul. However, about one thing Inge was sure of: she would do all within her possibility to legalize Uhuru's stay.

In Rome the weather was all together foul, raining for much of Saturday afternoon. It was certainly no weather that encouraged spending time window shopping and making purchases of outlandishly priced items. The concierge at their comfy hotel in Piazza Barberini assured them that the gray weather was unusual for Rome at this time of the year, and that this current uncharacteristic climatic manifestation, typical of northern Europe, was down to global warming. But that didn't comfort them much, since they had traveled this far with expectations of sitting outdoors, drinking cappuccino, and feeding pigeons in a plaza awash with spring sunshine. In spite of the rain, Inge and Annemarie determined to visit the fashionable Via dei Condotti stores.

They did quite some shopping, spending generously out of habit and not caring a straw. Inge thought of buying Uhuru an Armani boxer shorts, just for the fun, but dismissed that as an idea in bad taste, like giving one's lover a whoopee cushion on Valentine's Day. However, Annemarie thought the idea hilarious and found it a pity that Inge had changed her mind. They walked into a confectionery, ate some wonderfully delicious cakes, and drank cappuccino. Then there was time for

Annemarie to fret about Erozan, who was staying with Henk Koopmans. When Inge felt she had had enough of Erozan for a day, she suggested they walk to the jewelers. They spent quite some time in the store, searching for an appropriate jewelry present for Uhuru.

"This will certainly thrill him, won't it?" Inge asked, as the shop assistant packed Uhuru's present.

"Oh, darling," Annemarie said with genuine enthusiasm, "a perfect gift for a young lover. That will make a nice surprise for him. I wouldn't mind spending hundreds of euro on a man like Uhuru. The problem is that I need to find one, and quick!" There were warm smiles on their lips, smiles that couldn't be wiped off by the foul weather as they stepped out into the ever bustling street.

On Sunday the weather hadn't improved much but Inge and Annemarie, despite not being religious in any way and certainly without any form of affinity to Catholicism, braved the drizzle and stood with thousands in Piazza San Pietro to receive the Pope's weekly blessings, after which he waved his ecclesiastical authority upon the pilgrims. The sight of the ailing Pope evidently struggling to show his appreciation to the faithful greatly moved Inge, and she was at a loss to find a connection between the improvement of the weather and the Pope's blessing. For while standing in the square, the gray clouds had dissipated, giving way to a sun-drenched Rome spring redolent with the luster of ancient charm. Annemarie said it was just one of those lucky coincidences but Inge saw in the rejuvenated sunshine the invisible hand of a metaphysical force, a sign of the divine. The rest of their stay in Rome was filled with sunshine, and they went to the Colosseum and other ancient ruins, visited the Vatican museums and generally walked about, sniffing the Renaissance, as Inge remarked. They had time, and plenty of it, to share secrets in conspiratorial notes, murmuring excitedly and giggling, as if they were little girls. And on Monday evening after dinner, they sat in Inge's room drinking red wine, the finest Trabucchi Amarone if the hotel was to be believed. Annemarie was now confiding to a puzzled Inge how she felt about Henk Koopmans.

"He is on the whole a lovable person, you know. He is been coming around quite a bit. Who knows, we might give it a try! In fact, I feel quite sure he would make a better husband than Paul. You should see him playing with Erozan! The dog has rather taken a liking to him. It was as if the two were made for each other, a perfect match." And Inge thought, yes, a perfect match for man and dog but not you and Henk.

"How come this sudden interest in Henk?"

"I figured out there was no point living without a man. And Henk was there, waiting. If you know what I mean ... it is not like you have changed your mind and still want to give him a chance, is it, my dear?" She turned to Inge suddenly.

"I am perfectly happy with Uhuru," Inge said emphatically to put Annemarie's heart to rest. Annemarie's current interest in Henk did not bother her in the least. In fact, she welcomed it as good riddance from the man. She would not be obliged to sit next to him at parties anymore. That will be Annemarie's duty, forthwith, she thought with joyous relief.

"When are you two shagging? Can't wait to hear the juicy details!" Annemarie laughed, raising the wine glass to her lips.

"If that decision was solely on my shoulders, then Uhuru and I should have consummated our love a long time ago," Inge's eyes were afire from both the wine and thoughts of Uhuru.

Annemarie's eyes twinkled with naughtiness. "Believe me, girl. It is quite fascinating and satisfying. And I do speak from experience, mind." It is then that she told Inge about the Gambian escapade in all its spicy details and unfettered eroticism thus confirming what had only been a rumor, although most people, including Inge, had always held a deep conviction that the encounter had inevitably happened.

Uhuru was never far in their conversations, and now Inge decided time was ripe to seek advice on how best to deal with legalizing her lover's stay in the Netherlands. She had entertained thoughts of marrying Uhuru if it took that to obtain his residency permit and thus not lose him. However, upon further reflection, she decided that was quite out of the question, since she would be forcing him to commit bigamy, an offense before the law. Two wrongs, she knew, didn't make a right. So she let that thought pass.

"Well," Annemarie said, after pondering long and deep, "you could confine him to the attic, away from any prying eyes of the law. It has been done in the past, and with success!"

"But there is a sad end, most of the times," Inge said slowly. "A mole that gives the secret away, isn't it? Poor Anne Frank!"

"Right, my dear!" Annemarie said, as she filled her glass with wine, and then asking Inge, "More wine?" Inge nodded and Annemarie filled her glass, and they drank to the health of Inge and Annemarie. And then they drank to Uhuru, and then to the Gambian boy before finally remembering to drink to Henk Koopmans' health.

"You could get a smart lawyer to argue Uhuru's case. They are expensive though, but that is just a little inconvenience."

"Mr. Borowski?"

"He practices criminal law … a criminal lawyer. He certainly is one of the best in the country but not good for your purposes."

"Any cunning minds out there that you would recommend?"

"You need an immigration lawyer." Annemarie's face furrowed in thought. "The problem is I do not know of any. I wasn't subversive enough to bring that Gambian young man home, for if I had we would not be reinventing the wheel!"

Then Annemarie remembered the government's special amnesty program to grant residency permits to over two thousand asylum seekers and other illegal aliens.

"Perhaps Uhuru should apply for the amnesty," Annemarie said excitedly.

"What must he do, then?" Inge thoughtfully sipped her wine.

"Go to City Hall, I suppose."

"City Hall? What has Uhuru's stay got to do with City Hall?"

"That is where he registers for the general pardon ... the amnesty for all the illegal residents, you know. It is on the television news almost hourly, and I honestly begin to tire of the opposing sides in this debate. Some of the freakish things that they scream out are outright terrifying, almost like the 1930s and 40s. Anyway, Uhuru should register for the amnesty."

The idea was appealing, and Inge promised that as soon as they were back in the Netherlands she would instruct Uhuru to make haste to register with City Hall. She was convinced he shouldn't have a problem getting a residency permit, and Annemarie thought as much. After all, the women reasoned, Uhuru was employed by a law-abiding, wealthy resident of Kralingen who never failed to pay her taxes that was the highest form of civic duty. In that respect, Inge and Annemarie concluded, Uhuru, more than any other illegal immigrant out there, qualified for the Netherlands residency permit. Inge was so grateful for her friend's advice and glad that she had not canceled their trip to Rome.

Uhuru had learned to deal with his friends' bullying in the matter of his relationship with Inge. In fact, he had already admitted that he was in love with the woman, stressing that his affection for Inge had nothing to do with her legendary wealth. Pierre, Greg and Amadu were at the apartment when Uhuru told them of the expensive dinner at *Klomp & Tulip*. They listened to him in wondrous amazement and couldn't conceal their envy. Then Uhuru had told them of Inge's promise to see to it that he acquired a residency permit.

"You see," Greg burst forth with self-righteous excitement, "we told you! That woman is well connected to the relevant people. I wish I could know how she will handle this residency permit thing."

"Perhaps she plays golf with politicians that could pull one or two strings," Amadu said. "If the politicians happen to be of the right-wing hue and aghast at having one more immigrant, then she can always turn to bribing. She has enough quid to bribe the entire bunch at Immigration and Naturalization Department!"

"There is no corruption in this country," Uhuru interjected. Very often he struck a nationalistic tone in his defense of the country's institutions.

"What about the corruption scandals that we read about, eh?" Amadu questioned, amused by Uhuru's blindness in face of contrary evidence.

"Yes, Uhuru," Pierre added. "The recent well-publicized shenanigans of the construction industry and the disgraceful kickbacks. What do you have to say to that dude? What about that racket of self-enrichment at some of the ministries? Promoting cronies and making fictitious payments that no doubt end in Swiss bank accounts. If that is not corruption, then I need a psychiatric examination."

"But that is different," Uhuru began.

"No!" Amadu shouted. "I hate that phrase, "that is different" or worse, "you are different." Have you ever heard someone uttering profanities directed at your culture, but hurriedly adding that it didn't really apply to you. since you are quite different, or more specifically rather similar to them? Do you want me to go on? Anyhow, there is corruption in this country as well. The only difference between here and back home is that the judicial machinery works, some times. There is a system of checks and balances, and if you are caught you are strafed. Period. Now it doesn't matter if you are Bolkestein, the European Commissioner living high on the hog in Strasbourg, or Stein van Bolke, the mason down the road."

Whereas Inge had timed her Rome trip to coincide with Queen's Day celebrations as a way of escaping the frenzy that gripped the nation at that time of the year, Uhuru's response to the royal festivities was one of anticipation and high expectation. He had risen early to hang the Dutch national flag on the balcony rail. Then he had draped himself in orange, the national color: orange wig, orange tee-shirt, orange trousers and orange wooden shoes. When Greg and Pierre came into the living room much later they found Uhuru attentively following the royal procession on television.

Greg laughed hard at Uhuru's orange outfit. "You look like some outrageous imitation of a clown."

"Bassie and Adriaan," Pierre said. Uhuru's comical figure reminded him of the famous children's clown and acrobat pair.

Uhuru ignored their mean remarks, reveling in his orange paraphernalia.

"The Queen's helicopter landed about four minutes ago in Poederdorp," he announced to his housemates with gusto, eyes glued to the television. "That is the mayor walking besides the Queen. And his wife, I believe … she is the one with the orange plumes on her hat."

"Poederdorp?" Greg echoed in deep thought. "Isn't that Inge's hometown?"

"Yeah," Uhuru said. "Imagine she has missed this unique opportunity to see the Queen in her hometown. I would give anything to see the Queen in Rotterdam!"

"Ah, stop fretting over your girlfriend!" Greg said. "She is entitled to some fun in Rome if that brings her happiness more than a royal visit to her hometown."

"If I were you, I would be excited about her Rome trip," Pierre said. "Who knows what presents she might bring back for you from the eternal city? I gather it is the home of fashion."

Greg laughed loudly and with an element of malice. "Yes, perhaps she will replace your famous Mandela shirt with an Armani suit!"

"I do love her, and it is not about her ability to give me presents," Uhuru said defensively.

"Let's be honest," Greg pressed, "the money has its allure, doesn't it? *Klomp & Tulip* and Armani suits do not come cheap or do they?"

"That is mean," Pierre said, as he came to Uhuru's rescue. He had seen a flicker of hurt in Uhuru's eyes. "We shouldn't grudge Uhuru a rich woman. Care for a cigarette, dude?" Pierre extended a cigarette packet to Uhuru. Uhuru shook his head.

He had decided to dispense with the habit, to free himself from nicotine addiction in order to stand in his employer's good books. Keeping a job was far more satisfying than inhaling smoke, he had reached the conclusion. Besides, the smoke killed, and the job sustained life. Uhuru didn't regret his choice which had been tough in the beginning. Anyhow, the worst period of craving for a dose of nicotine in his circulation was over, and he doubted if he would ever revisit the habit. And now the television viewers were shown a brass band of men and women clad in traditional Dutch costumes playing the Wilhelmus, and tears of emotion welled in Uhuru's eyes as he sang the national anthem. He didn't pay particular attention when Greg stood, turned away from the television, and declared that Latasha was moving in with Goran.

"I should have laid her long ago," Greg said wistfully, as he walked to the kitchen to toast bread for his breakfast. At this, Uhuru remarked that there was more to life than laying women.

The evening of Inge's scheduled return from Rome found Uhuru glued to the television. He could not go to bed until he had read on Teletext that Inge's flight had landed safely. The next morning he headed to House of Java, making sure to walk into the florists, to buy a surprise for Inge. What he had really wanted was to give her a special present; a set of golf clubs. Although the thought was noble, the cost was prohibitive, way beyond his financial means. It was thus that he had settled for something cheaper, but equally endearing, nonetheless. He bought a bouquet of flowers with yellow, purple, and green spring blossoms, colors abundant in the garden at House of Java and which he assumed would please Inge. This was the first time that he had bought flowers for anybody in the Netherlands, and it thrilled him. It didn't matter that the flowers cost him a whopping fifteen euro, the amount of money he previously didn't think worth spending on a teddy bear for his daughter. At House of Java, he walked around to the rear of the house and knocked on the kitchen door (Inge had given him the key to the kitchen door for purposes of watering the indoor plants. But he thought it rude to ease himself into the house unannounced; too much show of familiarity). As Uhuru waited for the door to open, he ran a hand through his hair and looked at the flowers in his hand. He wondered how she was going to receive the present.

Presently, Inge opened the door, and Uhuru saw before him a woman with a more youthful vitality. Her hair was in a bun, and she was barefooted. She was dressed in a dark blue robe of pure satin silk. Uhuru was speechless, as he stood admiring that feminine figure of exquisite desirability. Inge's presence distracted him from the discomfort of grit lodged in his left shoe whilst walking about the gravel path to House of Java. He would worry about that later, when inspecting his sore blistered sole in the evening. They exchanged greetings and said how they had missed each other. Then Uhuru handed her the flowers. Inge was overwhelmed and profoundly touched by his gesture, and she let a tear or two run down her cheeks.

Uhuru took in her cleavage. "I missed you, Inge."

"Me too, my love." She was acutely aware of his eyes on her, hungry for her body.

"And I thought a lot about you, every minute."

"It is so nice of you to think of me," she said and studied the beautiful flowers. "Thank you, darling." She gave Uhuru the inevitable and customary three kisses – two on his left and one on his right cheek. She said it was very decent of him to give her flowers. And just as Uhuru's blood began boiling with adventure, a desire to prolong the early morning intimacy, he caught sight of a face behind Inge, standing in the doorway that adjoined the kitchen and the dining room. Uhuru could not believe his eyes! It was the same shop assistant that had trailed him at House of Snygrens, and the very woman he had encountered in his apartment block!

"My niece," Inge said, by way of introduction, and then, "Katrine, will you place these beautiful flowers for me on the working top? I want to have a word with Uhuru." She handed the flowers to Katrine who accepted them with a show of little emotion. Inge stepped into a pair of dainty sandals. They walked side-by-side on the cobblestone path from the kitchen to the tool shed. He inquired about her trip, and she said Rome was simply divine. "We must go there together, as soon as your papers are in order," she said indulgently. She looked back, as if to make sure that Katrine was out of hearing range. Then she told Uhuru about Katrine and her beastly husband. Katrine had rang her the previous evening, soon after her return from Rome. "She was in pain and crying. That brute had been beating her again. Slammed her head into the wall and threatened to kill her. I asked her to drive over and spend some few days with me."

"Why can't she abandon the man?" Uhuru asked with righteous indignation. He was thinking how odd it was that the strong sense of independence which manifested itself in the form of total disinterest in neighbors somehow did protect abuse of this nature. He somehow suspected Katrine's immediate neighbors in the apartment block must have known of the abuse but chose silence in the name of not interfering into other people's affairs. And it was so odd, when he contemplated further, that these same neighbors were perfectly in a state to ring the police about a black man in their neighborhood with an expensive car, and one that they wished to see quizzed about his source of income. Uhuru felt a sense of pity for Katrine.

"Well, we have all suggested that she divorces the man. She maintains that she is madly in love with Jan Willem." She shrugged her shoulders and shook her head in disbelief.

"Romantic folly, I guess," Uhuru said. He knew what dumb love was capable of unleashing, driving people to commit their affections unconditionally and against all common logic.

Inge deliberately kicked a pebble on the cobblestone path. "I guess that is what it is. She has this constant fear that if she leaves him, then she will be all alone, vulnerable. She told me last night that she didn't believe in divorce that I thought was quite brave for one that is even not a Catholic! But we should forget her vicissitudes for a moment."

Inge cordially steered the conversation away from her traumatized niece. "I brought you a little something, darling."

She removed a gift paper wrapped little box from the pocket of her robe. Uhuru was speechless as he opened the box, praying it was not an engagement ring of sorts. Yes, he did love Inge with all his heart, but again, he loved Mapenzi equally. He didn't want to betray her by abandoning their marriage, even if they hadn't seen each other for all these years. He still had fond memories of his wife. But again, if Inge were to drive him to a point where he would be forced to choose between his job and Mapenzi, then he simply didn't know the best course of action, he was all nerves and muddled up. Slowly, doing a good job to steady trembling fingers, he removed the gift wrap paper and flipped the box open. It was a gold chain!

"Is it something you care about?" Inge's eyes smiled. She was thinking of him lying on the beach, beside her naked body.

"Simply stunning!" Uhuru gasped. He was breathless with excitement. "I wouldn't know how to thank you, Inge."

"Well, just teach me the salsa or some tribal African dance!" She laughed heartily.

"As a matter of fact, I do not know how to dance," Uhuru said, as he recalled the night he had bumped into Goran.

Inge laughed. "Never mind, we can both learn." Then she reclaimed the chain from him and clasped it round his neck. When she was done, Uhuru grabbed her with a hungry urgency, kissing her on the lips.

"No, not now!" Inge whispered, as she gently pushed away from him. "I can't wait, too, but it has to be later, when she has left." They looked at each other longingly and laughed. Uhuru and Inge felt that they had found everlasting happiness, the elusive eternal bliss.

—

In the afternoon, she went out to the garden and told Uhuru what she had discussed with Annemarie in Rome. "You should go to City Hall tomorrow and register for the amnesty. I can't see them disqualifying you." Then she said it would be wonderful if Uhuru brought his friends over for coffee one of these days. She wanted to get to know them, and especially get to listen to Amadu recite his philosophical poems.

"You will write me a poem too, won't you, Uhuru?" she asked with excited intensity. Before he could respond, she said wistfully, "A little African poem riddled with sunshine and graceful animals hopping about the savannah!" Then she laughed as if amused by her ability to fantasize. He laughed, too, and promised he would write her a poem, a love song.

"*Lekker ding!*" she said fondly. She said Katrine was probably sleeping and invited Uhuru indoors. They drank coffee and listened to classical music, Tchaikovsky's violin concerto. Inge inquired if he would rather listen to something else. He said he was fond of classical music, as well, and Tchaikovsky captured the romantic mood of that moment. Indeed, he loved classical music, and he often had to come to its defense when his housemates and friends, unrepentant *soukous* aficionados, spoke disparagingly about it, stressing its lack to ignite passionate salvos that energized bodies to dance with abandon. Latasha once famously declared that only one lacking a rhythmic predisposition could appreciate this affront to the ears. Uhuru had defended the finesse of the music, its scientific sophistication that relegated the sounds of the African djembe to a primeval sonorous age of rumbling chaos, a time when the earth was just emerging after the Big Bang. But Latasha had maintained that Western classical music sounded as if someone had decided to play *soukous* in reverse sequence, beginning from the end and ending at the beginning.

Inge said she had offered to go off with Katrine on a short holiday. Just to calm her nerves, she said.

"I hate being separated from you, especially after missing you for the last days," Inge said sincerely. "But I also have responsibilities to my niece. She will not listen to her parents, and I am probably the only person that can help her at this time, her hour of need. It is better that she spends a quiet time away from Rotterdam."

"Are you taking her to Rome?"

"We are going to Zeeland, in the south. I do have a lovely vacation home there, a short walk from the sea. We've got to go down there together sometime."

"It is so kind of you to take her away from all the stress." Uhuru was genuinely touched by Inge's show of warmth towards others and her deep sense of empathy for those in need.

"I hope you don't mind, darling," she said, her voice pleading. "We are leaving tomorrow."

"By all means do everything it takes to help her out of her trauma," Uhuru said honestly.

"Thanks for your understanding," Inge said, sounding relieved. "We'll be gone for a few days, though. Back on Sunday. Oh, I'll miss you so!"

"Same here." Uhuru's eyes brightened with romantic excitement.

"Don't forget the City Hall tomorrow, okay?" she reminded.

"First thing in the morning, I guarantee."

"I am positive it will work out, and if not, there will be other means," Inge said with a sense of deep conviction. Then at that point, she thought of turning to Gerda. She knew that Gerda, more than anybody else, had the political clout and network to ensure that Uhuru was granted a residency permit. But on realization that she had not shown much enthusiasm to Gerda's crusade and had politely declined to sign Gerda's letter petitioning parliament in the matter of the inhumane treatment of unaccompanied minor asylum seekers, Inge doubted if she could count on Gerda for support. If City Hall wasn't forthcoming and the worst came to the worst, she reasoned that she might have to swallow her pride and solicit Gerda's support after all.

When Katrine, looking paler and more melancholic than ever, walked into the room some minutes later, Uhuru thanked Inge for her generous hospitality and took his leave. He thought it best to give them enough room and privacy to discuss their Zeeland holiday.

—

Frank Hogenhuizen couldn't stand rejection. He felt humiliated by Inge's rebuff and sought to punish her, to teach her a lesson. Nobody dared treat him the way that bitch had done and expected to get away with it! He was a man that had come to believe that other people inhabited the world to do his will. And one such fellow that had been loyal over the years was Joost Zwarts, at that moment sharing a glass of sherry with Frank in his downtown Rotterdam office, an intimidating edifice with marble floors. It was midmorning, and the two men were in their second bottle of sherry.

"So you believe she has a love affair with this nigger boy, a gardener?" Frank asked, hatred and impatience biting deep into his inner core. Glass of sherry in hand, he left his chair and walked over to the window, looking outside at the sprawling city with its traffic and pedestrians. In the distance was the Rotterdam mast, towering above the city's skyline. He gawked at it, as if seeing it for the first time in his life.

"Positive about that, sir," Joost said with arms folded in total obedience.

"I did invite her to dinner, and she turned me down," he said with controlled anger. "The nigger comes around, and the trollop can't wait to take him to *Klomp & Tulip*! For all I know, he has been fucking her, and she has probably re-written her will, bequeathing all that Marc worked so hard for to that nigger bastard, a know-nothing, a nobody! I have never trusted that woman. I could shoot her myself, Joost." Overwhelmed with rage, he drained his glass of sherry before proceeding, "Deceitful, treacherous, manipulative, untrustworthy ... *verdorie*, I hate all women in this world! She must be hit where it hurts most! Do you hear me Joost! *Verdorie*, I want to see blood spilled in the Rotterdam streets."

Through this tirade, Joost remained cool and surgical. "We shall follow the usual procedure sir. Unless you want things executed differently this time, sir."

Frank's tone of voice was colder than the south-west wind in winter. "I like the standard approach, and no word to a soul,

166

okay?" Not that it was necessary to repeat these words of caution to Joost, a veteran of a dozen or so missions successfully conducted on Frank's behalf.

"No word to a soul, sir," Joost said with the chilling civility of a Nazi concentration camp guard.

"Okay, that settles it then." Frank emptied the remaining sherry in the bottle into his empty glass.

"You leave that to me, sir." Joost stood up to leave the office.

"And one more thing, Joost." The hint of menace in Frank's tone stopped the younger man in his stride.

Joost snapped to attention. "Yes, sir?"

"That ponytail makes you look like a woman, and I hate those damn tennis shoes you are wearing! *Verdorie*, Joost, do get something decent for your feet and visit a hairdresser!"

"Yes, sir!" Joost answered meekly.

And as Joost closed the door behind him, Frank wondered why he had never taken an interest in bedding him. Perhaps his manner of dress and that stupid ponytail, he reflected.

Back at Prof. A.S. van Vredeman apartment Uhuru's friends were ecstatic when he showed them the gold chain. It was immediately removed from his neck and passed around for them to fondle and admire. How they envied him profoundly!

"Now the investment is beginning to pay off," Pierre declared.

"Next will be that Armani suit, dude!" Washington Keya enthused.

Amadu examined the chain, fitted it on his own neck before passing it back to Uhuru. "Pawn the thing, dude. I know a place in downtown Amsterdam where they would give you a fortune for those gems. They also polish blood diamonds, just in case someone amongst us has some dirty looking stones." But Amadu was half-stoned from smoking marijuana, and Uhuru just looked at him with hostile eyes and said nothing; he didn't think much of the poet's counsel. How could he part with this powerful symbol of everlasting love? Over his dead body!

Later that evening after Amadu and Washington Keya had left, Uhuru and his housemates were seated in front of the television. Then in the middle of a rather uninspiring Dutch Sitcom, Uhuru told them of his intentions to register for amnesty. But this piece of news was met with an air of general disbelief. The conversation that followed was of a tone aimed at dissuading Uhuru from going along with Inge's proposal, however good-intentioned it sounded.

"I thought that Inge would call the mayor's private residence and make arrangements for a residency permit or even a Dutch passport! But this …" Greg stammered his disappointment, "… well, I didn't envisage such a development."

Uhuru's housemates argued that for all its bravery pursuing amnesty was a foolhardy enterprise, one that would end up in disaster. Not only would it have negative and wholly unwanted effect upon him but it would also expose Greg, his landlord for some years now, to a stiff financial penalty for harboring an illegal alien. Besides, sub-renting was punishable by city laws and those breeching this edict risked a hefty penalty, which Greg could ill afford.

"You should realize," Greg warned, "the world has changed drastically since the end of the Second World War. One risking everything to harbor the hunted is no longer looked upon as a hero. Offering shelter to an illegal alien is not a heroic deed anymore, believe me. The days of our beloved Anne Frank are gone, *finito!*"

"I entirely agree with Greg here, but I would like us not to lose perspective. Is Inge accompanying you to City Hall? If the answer is a reverberating yes, then it is a risk worth taking," Pierre said.

"Well," Uhuru said with determined forcefulness, "I am man enough to go to City Hall on my own. I don't need Inge for that."

Greg shook his head. "You are walking into a lion's den, friend."

"Are you going to walk in there and announce to all and sundry, 'Hey dudes, I am an illegal alien in orange wooden shoes and orange wig, and I am here to talk to that fat-assed mayor.' You then expect the harassed civil servant to rush you upstairs to the mayor's chambers," Pierre said and laughed sarcastically. "Tell you what! As soon as the guys at City Hall discover you are an illegal alien, and a black man at that, they will rub their hands in glee, salivating like hungry cats about to leap on a mouse with fractured legs and a broken spine. Next thing, you will be in handcuffs like some hardcore criminal, the kind that execute people in the streets of Amsterdam!"

"You guys exaggerate," Uhuru said, ever so eager to follow Inge's instructions, even if it meant risking life and limb. That woman loved him and could not lead him into the jaws of death. It was unthinkable.

"Exaggerate!" Greg re-echoed. "Ask Amadu's friend. The chap was from the Horn of Africa, if I recall. He was done in by the City Hall fellows. He presented himself at City Hall like a gazelle before a merciless lion, explaining that he had come to take advantage of the amnesty that the government had extended to all illegal aliens. Weren't the fellows so happy! Before he could get a response from the sweet smiling woman at the Civil Affairs Department he was surrounded by a team of unsmiling men and women of the Royal Netherlands Military Constabulary dressed in antiriot gear. The next day he was on the plane to Addis Ababa or Mogadishu, I don't recall which was which."

"This amnesty thing is a right-wing conspiracy," Pierre said, "a ploy to smoke out illegal aliens for deportation. Western governments do that all the time."

Uhuru refused to be intimidated by stories of deportation. The next morning he bathed, shaved, and dressed up in his Mandela shirt and a pair of Levis jeans (the Dockers had been washed and were on the balcony line drying). The golden chain around his neck brought a feeling of closeness to Inge, giving him a certain confidence and strength to carry out a mission his housemates had beseeched him to abandon.

City Hall was teeming with people when Uhuru made his entrance at nine thirty, which was his first in this hitherto menacing edifice of power and bureaucracy. After a moment of hesitation orientating himself in the vastness of City Hall with its numerous counters, Uhuru identified the automatic ticketing machine. He walked to the machine, cautiously pressed the green button and got his queue number ticket. As he waited for his number to be called, he studied the men, women, and children from all walks of life and of all colors that had come to City Hall. There were men with clean shaven heads in training suits looking as if they had just walked in from a far right wing demonstration. One woman, dressed in a burqa, was totally covered from head to foot, defying any further scrutiny. Half-fascinated he studied the numerous black faces wearing martyred expressions or airs of forced confidence. There were Oriental looking faces subdued in absolute humility. One mustached, bulky, white man built like a bodybuilder bent over and parted a crying child in the arms of a homely woman wearing a hijab. A well-dressed man, in navy blue suit and tie with a briefcase by his side, devoured an apple with singular ravenousness, as if survival in the remaining years of his life depended on that one fruit. All in all, there was an air of cheerfulness about these residents of Rotterdam as they patiently waited their turn to be served. Uhuru was pleased with this show of diversity, and he hoped it could only bring strength to this vibrant city that he so loved, and very much wanted to be part of. Then he reflected as to the reasons that had led these people to leave the comforts of their homes to seek the services of the Civil Affairs Department of City Hall. Uhuru surmised that some might be here to inquire about dog registrations or seek unemployment benefits. Perhaps others had come for debt counseling or probably had come to renew passports or driving permits. Which of these people, Uhuru wondered, had come to City Hall to register a birth or death, and which of them sought a housing subsidy or building permit?

When his number came up, he walked to a desk and stood before a redheaded plump middle-aged woman with long lashed blue eyes. Face twitching with nervousness he did his best to explain the purpose of his visit. But the woman had a problem making sense out of what he was saying. She had never heard of an amnesty for illegal aliens and didn't seem to make much of the knowledge that Uhuru was an illegal alien. All she knew, she said, was that the city was rather keen to banish poor immigrants from Rotterdam and disperse them to other cities.

"Rotterdam is only interested in opening its gates to new immigrants making at least twenty percent above the minimum wage," she said and eyed the gold chain hanging from Uhuru's neck; her own neck was a showcase of lovely pearls. "They must also be able to speak comprehensible Dutch. I do not think that you are disqualified under that score. Your Dutch is quite impressive and almost native level." And she said this not in an insultingly patronizing way but rather like she was stating a fact of life that shouldn't sound as if it was higher arithmetic to the innumerate. Uhuru earned just under the minimum wage.

"But how do I go about applying for this general amnesty or residency permit?" asked Uhuru bravely.

"Don't ask me!" the woman said good-humoredly. "Perhaps the Alien Police or better still, the Immigration and Naturalization Department people; they should know better than we mortals here at City Hall. If you like, I can give you their address. If you want a passport renewal, then you are at the right place." She flashed a disarming smile. Uhuru had expected to encounter passionate hatred and not this humane treatment. Listening to his housemates the previous evening, it seemed that he would be walking to inevitable harassment, unavoidable persecution, at the hands of civil servants with a determined hostility to run aliens out of town. He couldn't help wondering if this kindly-looking lady before him was running with the hare and hunting with the hounds. Was she making a special effort at being social towards the unfortunate soul that he was as she bade time for the men in antiriot gear to arrive? He doubted it. The smile, the slight inclination of the head to the right, the bright blue eyes convinced Uhuru that she conducted herself in good faith. There was nothing about her to even suggest the over-inflated airs of a half-illiterate drill-sergeant, something he had somehow come to associate with civil servants.

"Do not bother with the address, madam," he said politely.

"Anything else I can do for you today?" she asked with friendly interest.

"No thanks. Good day, madam."

Uhuru had no intention of going to the Alien Police offices or to the Immigration and Naturalization Department; the game wasn't worth the candle. Besides, Inge had not given him those instructions, and he still believed that if he was to get a residency permit then it would only happen through her intervention. Inge knew much better than he did, and Uhuru surmised that she was better placed to navigate through this complex maze of officialdom.

—

When Uhuru left City Hall and joined the hurrying crowd in the streets of Rotterdam, he could not help thinking of the kind redhead at City Hall. True, he had been rather apprehensive when he stepped into City Hall and had even wondered if he shouldn't take the advice of his housemates and avoid the building all together. The sun was obliterated behind white fluffy clouds, and there was a chilly wind that reminded him of the folly of having left his windbreaker at home. Nonetheless, his gaze brightened with relief at leaving City Hall, not as a prisoner restrained in handcuffs, but as a dignified free man, albeit an illegal alien. He was happy to be part of this fascinating city where he remained anonymous. He found his thoughts carrying him to Mapenzi. He mused about time flying and resolved to send her a letter, one that would be scrawled in tenderness and clothed in undying love. He resolved to write to her that evening. Perhaps he could send her a nice present, too, a dress or a delightfully scented perfume. Yes, he would buy that adorable teddy bear for Juliana as well. He could post the package on the weekend. But now it was time to return to work, to his gardening. As he sat in the tram, he wondered about Inge's next step in obtaining for him that valuable residency permit. Would she ask him to go to the Alien Police? Or would she insist that he sees the Immigration and Naturalization Department people perhaps? He resolved to obey whatever instructions and directions that Inge would provide.

When he got off the tram, he was again confronted by thoughts of Mapenzi and wondered if she had changed much in all these years. The photos that she had recently sent suggested the years had barely left a visible mark on her. Her face was still youthful and the charming smile alluring as ever. He turned left into President J. F. Kennedy Drive. He wondered why anybody in their right mind would have ever wanted to assassinate a well-meaning man. Then he was reminded of Kennedy's now immortalized words, *Ich bin ein Berliner.* Yeah, he thought good-humoredly, *Ich bin ein Rotterdamer!* Uhuru stepped aside to allow a jogger go past. If he ever got that residency permit, he reflected, he would make it a point to run the Rotterdam Marathon. That idea would bemuse Inge and send Mapenzi in a frenzy of excitement, he smiled. There was a cheerfulness that suffused his body, a joie de vivre of wholesomeness warmed his heart, and he found himself whistling. He whistled to the tune of *Oranje boven,* a song about the everlasting supremacy of the royal house, a melody in praise of the orange color, a symbol of national pride. But he didn't consciously recognize it as such, his mind preoccupied with how lucky he was to have met Inge Baleman-Ruyter, a woman that would soon remove him from the obscurity of illegality and lift him to heights he had never contemplated even in the wildest of his dreams. Yet, he wondered, could he ever feel comfortable in her kind of world, among the country's moneyed class and socialites? He couldn't quite imagine himself accompanying Inge to the golf club's annual dinner party in the mandatory black tie. He turned these considerations over in his mind, and the more he thought about it, the more uncertain he became about building a romantic relationship with Inge. Funny, he mused. He had come to the Netherlands with the conviction that a job, a good paying job at that, waited for him. His plans were basically simple. He would give Royal Chelloil his all and after five or six years retire to Uganda, back to his sweet Mapenzi and adorable Juliana. He hoped that by then, he would have saved enough money and accumulated adequate experience to set up an oil prospecting consortium in Uganda. He had studied the rock formation of the Lake Albert region, and he was convinced that the lake had more to offer than the giant Nile Bass. He put his right hand into the right pocket of his jean trousers, removed his wallet, and with the pride of a father looking at a daughter, he studied the chubby pink-cheeked Princess of Orange-Nassau.

—

Joost Zwarts had studied his quarry's routine for just a few days and concluded there would be no surprises. Uhuru always followed the same path each time he came to work. Why would he have cause to change his routine? Joost mused. Then he briefly wondered why Uhuru never bicycled to work. Perhaps he was too poor to buy himself a bicycle, Joost chuckled. This was going to be a simple operation, one hundred percent risk free. Who would care about the demise of an illegal alien? The fellow wasn't even a quantifiable statistic! How many illegal aliens lived in this country? Were they twenty thousand or two hundred thousand? As far as Joost Zwarts could recall, nobody seemed to have any idea, and he just didn't care. Therefore, common sense told him, nobody would surely be bothered by one subtracted from an uncertain statistics. The demise of an illegal alien would hardly send a ripple of outrage and might be welcomed as good riddance in quarters that currently held sway over political thought in the country. He just couldn't see those solemn marches of concerned citizens demonstrating in protest against senseless violence. Then Joost's thoughts darted briefly to his boss, dwelling on Frank's hatred of women. All of a sudden, he felt too warm in his gray striped Brixton suit, and he trembled in his tennis shoes; he had a secret affair with Sylvie, Frank's daughter. He was aware that if his boss ever came around to discovering the affair, that would spell the end of him; probably a shot through the head and the lifeless body stuffed into a barrel before being hauled to a final resting place at the bottom of the Rhine River.

Joost had been patiently waiting in a maroon Opel Kadett 1989 model for almost three hours in President John F. Kennedy Drive. He had simply eased the Opel between two other cars in a public parking area in the street. He now saw his quarry coming down the road. It didn't matter there were lots of people on the street; Joost was a good marksman. With cheerful malice, heart pumping with excitement, he tightened his finger on the DijkBlast 1445 automatic pistol, his favorite tool for the job at hand. It was debatable if Uhuru saw the gun aimed at him. Some witnesses at the crime scene swore that the dead man had raised his hands, as if to protest his innocence, but let them fall, perhaps in resignation at the inevitability of his demise. The look of panic in his face lasted just a fraction of a second, as it quickly was replaced by the more permanent horror of death. The police investigation that followed was swift. The police report concluded that the recent regrettable death of an illegal alien on President John F. Kennedy Drive was most probably a straightforward case of an unfortunate person caught in the crossfire of two feuding drug gangs. A Rotterdam newspaper account summarized the tragic event of Uhuru's demise rather differently.

Epilogue

After Uhuru's funeral, his friends were eager to invite Mapenzi to Rotterdam, to visit her husband's grave and pay her last respects. Mapenzi would have to go to the Netherlands embassy and fill in a visa application form, submit two passport-size photographs and show proof that she had a return air-ticket. Everything seemed to be going according to plan, and Pierre, much to everybody's surprise, managed to collect enough money for Mapenzi's air-ticket. "It is enough to bring Uhuru's daughter, as well," he boasted.

Greg took it upon himself to send a letter of invitation to Mapenzi and Juliana. In fact of all the people that were close to Uhuru in Rotterdam, he was the only one that would make such a commitment. Pierre would probably have volunteered, as well, but he didn't have a proper address, sub-renting as he was from Greg. One knowledgeable alien, a Sri Lankan gentleman of immense kindness, who had invited his mother once and could now claim some experience in matters of inviting aliens into the country, advised Greg that standard protocol required the letter of invitation to be duly signed and stamped by an official in City Hall.

"Make sure you make more than three copies of the stamped letter," the man had advised, and laughing, "My experience dealing with civil servants is that the more copies of stamped papers one has, the better."

At City Hall the redheaded lady, showing the same politeness she had extended to Uhuru earlier, advised Greg that he also needed to provide proof that he was not on unemployment benefits before inviting non-Western aliens into the country. He would also have to show that he earned enough money to provide for his visitor.

"What must I do to show proof of sufficient income?" Greg asked with irritation.

"Your pay-stubs for the last six months," said the redhead with much sympathy. She had been too long in the business that she could smell them if they lived on unemployment benefits.

"I see," Greg said resignedly.

"Anything else I can do for you today?" she inquired.

Greg felt like spitting at her but shook his head instead and left. He thought this one woman was the most insensitive person on the entire universe, and that if she had lived in an earlier age, she would probably have fitted in very well as a witch. If only, Greg reflected as he bicycled back to his apartment, if only he had a way of getting at that insolent woman, he would not hesitate to wring her neck. He felt the system marginalized him because of his race, a conviction now reinforced by the city's planned wall of Jericho, keeping out poor aliens. He hated all the white faces that he saw in the street that day, believing that they were part of a greater far-right wing conspiracy to make life a living hell for ethnic minorities. Why would anybody fail to see that a bereaving wife deserved a chance to mourn her husband? Mapenzi and Juliana would never come.

—

Inge returned from Zeeland feeling reinvigorated and with a sense of being in her twenties and not fifties. She couldn't wait to see Uhuru, to completely give herself to him. Katrine had yet again refused to abandon Jan Willem, and she was resolute that nobody should bring the matter of her bartering to the police's attention. Inge was utterly disappointed by her attitude, but thoughts of Uhuru and the romantic games that waited at House of Java helped to cheer her up. Uhuru, however, never turned up.

Two days after returning from Zeeland, a distraught Katrine came to House of Java unannounced and with her a copy of the *Rotterdam Weekly Herald*. The front page carried a photograph of a recently deceased man. Katrine had immediately recognized Uhuru's face and made haste to inform her aunt. Inge stared at Uhuru's photograph, at first uncomprehending.

Then she slowly read the accompanying text which detailed the motives of the violent demise of a one, Uhuru. The newspaper account portrayed Uhuru as a dangerous psychopath and seasoned hardcore criminal, a man that should not have been allowed to freely roam the streets of Rotterdam. The newspaper concluded that if crimes of a similar nature (unfortunately quite common these days) were to be contained and streets of the city reclaimed back to the city's peaceful citizens, then now was the time for politicians to stand up to their responsibility and introduce measures that would facilitate the quick rounding up and speedy deportation of all illegal aliens. And for good measure, the paper added that deportation must be the first option for all other non-Western aliens that didn't adhere to the norms and values of Western civilization.

"Sickening lies, *verdorie!*" Inge screamed, tearing up the newspaper. "An innocent, tender, and loving man of pure intention has been murdered, Katrine. Cold-blooded murder. Uhuru was an honest man and not a criminal. All he ever wanted to do was to work and look after his wife and child."

The cruelty and inhumanity of Uhuru's death weighed heavily on Inge, and she collapsed into the Jan des Bouvrie chair. Later that day, she sat in her living room studying the photographs of her late husband and Rianne, a child from her first marriage but one that Marc had treated as if she was his own flesh and blood. She thought how disgraceful it was that she didn't even have a photograph of Uhuru, no lingering memory save for the abyss of his absence that would remind her of those splendid and wonderful weeks when she felt young again!

About the Author

Robert Bwire is a physician who was educated in Uganda and the Netherlands, and he holds a Ph.D. from the University of Amsterdam. He currently lives in New Jersey. His scientific writings have appeared in numerous medical journals, and he is the author of two nonfiction books, *Bugs in Armor: A Tale of Malaria and Soldiering* and *Ashes of Faith: A Doomsday Cult's Orchestration of Mass Murder in Africa. Chain of Spring Love* is his debut novel.

CPSIA information can be obtained at www.ICGtesting.com
Printed in the USA
243995LV00002B/14/P